BUTTERFLY

BUTTERFLY

A NOVEL

JOHN DELACOURT

.ll.

Prepared for the press by Katia Grubisic
Cover design by Debbie Geltner
Author photo by Andrea Stewart
Book design by Tika eBooks
The lines from "Monologue for Cassandra" by Wisława Szymborska are reprinted by permission of Princeton University Press.
Printed and bound in Canada.

Library and Archives Canada Cataloguing in Publication

Delacourt, John, 1964-, author
          Butterfly : a novel / John Delacourt.

Issued in print and electronic formats.

ISBN 978-1-77390-012-4 (softcover).--ISBN 978-1-77390-013-1 (HTML).--
ISBN 978-1-77390-014-8 (Kindle).--ISBN 978-1-77390-015-5 (PDF)

          I. Title.

PS8607.E4825385B88 2019   C813'.6   C2018-905130-2
                                          C2018-905131-0

The publisher gratefully acknowledges the support of the Government of Canada through the Canada Council for the Arts, the Canada Book Fund, and Livres Canada Books.

Linda Leith Publishing
Montreal
www.lindaleith.com

… Now I remember distinctly
how people, on seeing me, stopped in mid-syllable.
Laughter broke off.
Hands pulled apart.
Children ran to their mothers.
I did not even know their evanescent names.
And that song about the green leaf—
no one finished it in my presence.

I loved them.
But I loved them from on high.
From above life.
From the future. Where it is always empty
and whence nothing is easier than to see death.
I regret that my voice was harsh.
Just look at yourselves from the stars, I called out,
just look at yourselves from the stars.
They heard me and lowered their eyes.

They lived in life.
Open to all the winds.
Foredoomed.
From birth in farewell bodies.
And yet in them was a certain moist hope,
a flame feeding on its own flickering.
They knew the value of the moment,
oh if but a single moment
before—

I told you so.
Except nothing follows from it.
And this is my fair garment singed by fire.
And these are my prophet's odds and ends.
And this is my contorted face.
The face that did not know it could be beautiful.

     Wisława Szymborska, "Monologue for Cassandra"

1. Lucien Bollinger

I don't believe in myths. I don't believe in bedtime stories about the afterlife either. Still, if there were ever a time for the one about a descent into the underworld to save the beloved, I suppose it would be now. Some myths have their moments.

I fell in love with Nataša Ružić at the Renzo Casale gallery, the night of Alex Rebane's opening. She walked out into the street as I made to leave and called my name. She kissed me, thanked me for coming, and I was hers if she wanted me. Point of no return.

She had been a student of mine for about a month. I found her attractive, but I had no interest in compromising my position as an instructor. The hours I was cobbling together amounted to the first decent work I had gotten since returning to Canada. My night classes in Parkdale were sparsely attended, but at least I could tell my supervisor no one was dropping out. The regulars were two nun-like sisters from Port-au-Prince who might have been twins, an older, well-dressed gentleman from Lvov who said he had been a jeweller (he wore a gold signet ring on his baby finger), and a short-order cook named Tran who sat near the back and kept his ski jacket on over his kitchen whites. Nataša showed up in the last week of March and took her place in the last seat of the last row. With her dyed black hair and her green leather jacket—surely a relic from the eighties—she had her own bold way of putting the glamour on. It was there with the eyeliner around her dark eyes, the sharp angle of her nose, the smile that showed a glimpse of sharp little teeth. She met my gaze that first night and her smile widened, even though she appeared self-conscious about her teeth and concealed them. She seemed to see something in me that was of interest, but then her eyes darted to the notebook in front of her. And when she spoke it was clear she was so far ahead of the others that I wondered why she was there, why she kept coming, week after week. I supposed it might have been a nightly escape from a one-room apartment nearby, a way not to be lonely for a while.

How could a woman like her be lonely?

Some weeks later, she waited until the others had filed out to approach my desk. She put down a shiny gallery card advertising an art show called Imperial Travesties.

"You like painting, Mr. Bollinger?"

I smiled, picked up the card. It was all I could do to say that I liked paintings a lot.

"You should come to the show. He's my friend."

Over the next week, prior to the opening, I did all the research I could on the artist, Alex Rebane. In the eighties, when I was still a kid, he had been huge, with shows in Manhattan, Berlin, and Tokyo, his paintings selling for six figures. He had real technique. He could paint a skinhead rally and the work would look like it had been on some rich man's wall in sixteenth-century Italy. But then he flamed out. The market went cold on him and he squandered his fortune, tried and failed and tried and failed to kick heroin, moved to Hamburg, then to Ubud, to Vancouver and then back to Toronto, finally clean. It looked like he was heading for a middle age of obscurity. The latest magazine profile reported that there was a time when no art dealer in Toronto would touch him anymore. But then something happened with his work and he was suddenly selling, suddenly something of a star again.

Maybe it was a maturing of his vision or maybe it was the times. This was after 9/11. The big money clients were seeking out more sober, contemplative, blue-chip investments, and Rebane began producing work on classical themes, stripped of all the too-clever postmodern tics like the split screens and the comic font he'd toyed with in the early nineties. He'd become cold-eyed, his crush on old masters turned almost noble. His work suddenly had all the ambition that the last vestige of a critic-driven market was looking for.

This man, this was Nataša's friend. Maybe nothing would come of us, but at the very least she could introduce me to an artist—or a community of artists—that I had been hoping to find in Canada after close to a decade in Tokyo. There I was, teaching newcomers, but it was me who still felt like an alien after two years in the city. Nataša, the quiet woman in the last row, held membership in a world where I wanted to belong.

I got my best dark suit cleaned, the one I hadn't worn since Japan, got my hair cut and, suitably transformed, splurged on a taxi to the gallery address on Ossington. I walked into the white-walled antechamber as the Bay Street and Forest Hill taxi fares had started to arrive. These were the tanned and silver-haired old millionaires browsing for investments, their younger second and third wives adorned in shimmering, interesting jewellery, a few character actors and pop singers who had had some good years working in America when they were thinner and not yet ravaged by various addictions and surgeries. This was a Toronto I got a cursory scan of in the society pages of the weekend papers, often contemptuously, as if here was visual evidence of how all the wrong people had the money and power in the city—not that I had any clue who the right people would be.

I was feeling nervous and out of place enough to walk out and have a cigarette in the street, but then I saw Nataša get out of a taxi with another couple. Her eyes widened and she gave me a big smile. For a moment I was no longer some awkward fool in the crowd. Maybe I could be different from them all, and different in the eyes of a beautiful woman.

But she was not going to fall into the moment the way I hoped she would. She turned and said something to the man and woman accompanying her. Friends? No, they were dressed too differently, the woman in a vermilion dress that, with her pale skin and long red hair, looked to be from another era. The man with her seemed so pleased with himself in his electric blue suit. Those two were on their own, staring into each other's eyes as if everyone around them were in soft focus. They were Caroline Vidler and Petar Stepanović and, out of jealousy for what I perceived as their wealth and their connections—and probably not least their affiliation with Nataša—I decided they were frauds.

As I followed them back into the gallery Nataša turned her back to me and spoke to the couple. There was a finality to her gesture, in accordance with the choreography of strangers compelled to move among each other, that she wanted to resist. She looked back at me once more. Her signal for me to introduce myself.

Petar Stepanović noticed. He looked at me as if through a window, staring out into the dark, trying to spot a prowler on the grounds. Nataša smiled and muttered something to him. Perhaps it was a way to reassure him that I was a marginal figure, best left in the background. Maybe Petar was an older brother. But no, why would he reach a hand out to the small of her back now and turn her away? I couldn't figure them out.

They walked into the largest room of the gallery and there, over their shoulders, I glimpsed the painting that made them stop. Caroline put a hand to her chest. The painting showed the head of a bearded man on a platter, a dwarfish figure presenting it to a woman who turned from the scene as if she could not bear to look. The woman in the painting, with her hair pulled back under a dark scarf, was unmistakable; it was Nataša.

I could not see Nataša's reaction, she was turned from me. I knew something was being revealed, something only these three knew about. These three and the painter, of course.

I realize now I should have followed them into that room, waited for an appropriate moment and introduced myself. I could have discovered what it all meant. And maybe that would have gone a long way to explaining what happened afterwards. But I walked out of the gallery and started to head home alone. There seemed such a secret, private language between Petar, Caroline, and Nataša and I couldn't see a point of entry. I had my face pressed up against the glass, looking in on a world I'd never know.

What a small amount of courage I had. Despite the distances I had travelled in my thirty years, all I had seen and tried to photograph, I still prized my innocence, my fear of what people who lived in the world of experience knew. People like Nataša ...

That might have been the end of the story if Nataša hadn't followed me out and pulled me back in to that night. She called my name, and I turned, defenceless.

2. Alex Rebane

Dear M.,

Well isn't this something, old friend. It looks like they have come around to me once more. Renzo has just emailed to say he has already sold five of the sixteen paintings in the show. Two of them went for double what I could get even two years ago. And the media's coming to the opening. Frank Owendyke from the goddamned *New York Times* is flying up. And Renzo swears he has nothing to do with that.

I remain unmoved. We both know what the current interest in my work is about. It is a bone thrown my way as a reward for all the money I'm making for a few people. I don't even begrudge Caroline Vidler or Barany or whoever else among the jackals they deal with who might have been instrumental in making this happen. The difference between the first time my work was selling well and now is that I understand that it's not about me, ultimately. I know exactly what I must do: play it out for as long as possible, bank the money until I have enough to tell them all I will not do their bidding any more.

We're both murderers, aren't we, old friend? Beyond rehabilitation. At least you never murdered your talent.

I'll write you again soon.

A.

3. Nataša Ružić: Notebook One

The time code says 2:17 pm/07/12/92. The day everything changed in a young girl's life. The woman I am now cannot return to where this episode took place to mourn because first there would have to be some forgiveness, some peace made with the past. To be there again and take in the silence would make what is familiar unbearably alien. I can only wander now, a stranger everywhere. There is no peace without justice.

The first image I see is a mountain road, then a line of men marching in single file. The camera shot comes into focus on them below the waist, the wild grass as high as their knees. The shot pulls up to take in the torsos, the shoulders, the faces of them all. They are dressed as though they've just come home from work. I see the postman I remember—Azmir, with only three fingers on one hand. There's Izet, the old man who had the newsstand by the train station, still wearing that Yankees baseball cap some tourist gave him. Some in the line look confused. A couple of older ones look defiant. Strangely, so few of them seem afraid.

Two soldiers walk beside these men. The first soldier in the frame looks barely old enough to have been conscripted, with his rosy cheeks and patchy blonde stubble. He is dressed in fatigues and a beret, awkwardly cradling his AK-47 in his arms like a child he'd rather disown. This is Dejan. He gazes down at the pavement, and—am I reading too much into his wide-eyed glare?—I imagine him realizing the implications of his orders. Behind him, another soldier comes into view. He is a little taller, dark-eyed, Turkish-looking, his face is so tanned from weeks of marching in the sun. This is Petar. He looks straight ahead, as if he is reluctant to acknowledge the humanity beside him.

There are other soldiers, spread out along the line of men, but they are not in focus. They will never have names, never fear discovery. But for those who do have names, I want to ensure a reckoning.

As the two soldiers in the frame wave their rifles, directing the line of men off the road into a clearing, a Jeep appears. The man driving is a blurry, sunglassed face behind the windshield, but his passenger is standing tall to take in the view. The man wears a costume from another time, with his feathered cap, epaulettes on his starched fatigues. The aviator sunglasses he's wearing only enhance the ridiculous self-important look on his face. This is Nikola. He gazes at the line of men, as if he were staring far beyond them, out into the greater horizon of historical moments to come, imagining his place there.

As the line of men file off camera into what looks like a meadow, the Jeep stops. Nikola steps out of the car, hikes his pants over his paunch and becomes, with his posture and his shuffle, unremarkable once again. He too exits the frame.

And then you can hear the shots, echoes of the last voices summoning the courage to curse or pray.

I stop the video. Forty-eight seconds. Not much there, but really, if you wanted to prosecute, there's more than enough. I point and click and play it one more time, even though one more time was supposed to be twenty minutes ago.

Soon, though, soon, I know I won't be able to take it anymore. And when I click on the clip for the final time, I promise myself I will never look at it again. The time has come for me to believe I can keep my word. And to seek justice.

This is how I am going to live. I'm never going to look back again once what I have to do is done.

4. Lucien Bollinger

The few months that followed, from the opening of Rebane's show until the night of the blackout in Toronto, were the happiest time of my life. I was in love, and I had reason to believe Nataša was falling in love with me.

"Come, Lucien Bollinger. Come and tell us who you really are." She invited me out the night that Alex's show opened, once she had caught up to me on the street. I was surprised that I could be mysterious to anyone, and that she had felt whatever secrets I might have had would be worth revealing. But she took my hand as if we were already a couple, and marched me back to the gallery. "Smile for me," she said. "You don't have to be shy."

Once we had returned she walked me through each room, explaining each painting to me. She told me what Alex had based each work on, what it had been like to pose for him, for hours, in the sweltering heat of his back studio. Flies buzzing around her that she couldn't swat. She could only break into the slightest grin while he chattered away over the opera CDs he would blare. Verdi was his favourite. The drama was so simple, so immediate, he had said. As I listened to her I could just nod; I was too self-conscious to speak about the paintings I liked or why.

"I want you to come with me to the restaurant where Alex is having his after-party. You can help save me from Caroline and

Petar. I used to work for them in Montreal before I came to Toronto. Will you do that for me?" She squeezed my hand and then said something I tried to laugh off, something I think about every day now. "You would make a terrible hostage. I can see everything you're feeling by the look on your face."

"Is that bad?"

"Not at all, Lucien Bollinger. It is one reason I chased you when you left the gallery."

Over more glasses of Barolo and the Neapolitan dishes that glided past us in Renzo Casale's favourite restaurant, the conversation I had with Caroline and Petar was far better than I had expected. Caroline laughed too loudly at any quip we overheard from Alex as he moved about the room. She managed to drop the names of a Saudi billionaire, a tennis player, and a pop singer within the first ten minutes of our conversation. She also seemed genuinely interested in getting to know who I was. She said Tokyo fascinated her (among a list of what fascinated her—it seemed a favourite verb) and wanted me to tell her what she absolutely-had-to-see if she went. As soon as I mentioned my photography she made me promise, if I and Nataša "became a thing," to show her my work. "But you should be a thing. You two look great together."

Petar was far more circumspect. He nodded and smiled when Caroline told me about their gallery in Montreal. She said that Alex was helping Petar land a show in Toronto. He leaned back and nodded knowingly. He was proud of how she promoted him, as if she were the front of the house and he were comfortable in the background. But the more Caroline drew me out, the more Petar's attention wandered. He engaged Nataša in a conversation in Serbian, but she was terse, more focused on Caroline and me, and it irritated him. He walked out for a cigarette, shrugging when Nataša declined his invitation for her to come along. I didn't think much of it at the time; we were men in a room where the competitive drive was badly concealed. The default response to a stranger was suspicion and contempt.

Near the end of the evening, Nataša brought me over to Rebane, out on the College Street corner where Alex was smoking, his empty glass of grappa perched on the curb. She introduced me as her new friend and Alex, his eyelids heavy, slurred, "I compliment you on your great taste, Mr. Bollinger." I tried not to be effusive, but I had also had too much to drink and saw no reason to hold back on how much I loved his paintings. He invited me to his house to see more, said now he was convinced I was a man with an eye for the truly beautiful. He winked at me, a parody of how straight men talked to each other.

When I left the restaurant, Nataša walked me outside. She said that she had not enjoyed herself so much with a guy in a very long time. When I kissed her, and asked if I might see her again, she gave the sidewalk a stern look, said, not quite seriously, that she would miss her evenings conjugating verbs in the Parkdale school. "Of course, Mr. Bollinger. I very much want to see you again."

She began to meet me on the evenings when we both were free. Neither of us had much money, which meant a drink or dinner in the bars and restaurants within walking distance of Alex's home and my apartment. The nights were warm, the streets that ran parallel from Alex's home near Queen and Bathurst to my apartment in Parkdale were full of such life, with the smell of smoke from the backyard barbecues, the thump of hip hop from fast cars, the cartoon colours of hopscotch games chalked up and then smudged and abandoned by dusk. With leaves on the trees and the front yard gardens in bloom with roses and hibiscus flowers, the neighbourhoods were no longer so stark and bleached out. I had forgotten what it was like to sit with a woman at a patio table, so enrapt that all else went out of focus but the space between us, the little still lifes of wine glasses, ashtrays and cigarettes.

There was so much to learn, so much I wanted to understand about her life. She told me that when she was young she had hoped to become an actor. "For the theatre, not the crap on TV." There was a family friend who was a director, and he had found her some work in Sarajevo. But first there was the war back home, which had interrupted her studies. Later, living in London, she said she had realized the limits of her talent. Petar was a friend she had met there. Yes, they had been lovers for a time. He was living in Montreal and suggested she come over, he could find her work. It was during her time as a gallery assistant for Caroline that she had met Alex. She had taken him up on his offer to model for him over the summer, and here she was.

Now that she no longer had any aspirations to be on stage, she said she wanted to figure out how to write. This was why she had shown up in my class; she had been in the public library and saw the ad for free classes and figured what did she have to lose? Her father had been a failed writer. Who knows, she said, laughing, maybe it ran in the family. If she had to choose between becoming a failed actor or a failed writer she would take the latter.

I was wary of a dynamic I had fallen into with my ex, Keiko, when we were living together in Tokyo. I had become the transitional figure, the bridge between one part of her life and another. Once that bridge of learning the language was crossed, her adventure as an émigré awaited on the other side. Adventure without me.

I had to make this clear. I told Nataša that working with words was a means of making a living for me back in Canada, and a poor living at that. Images were really all I cared about. Powerful, dramatic images, no kitsch. That is why I immediately fell in love with Alex's work. It was rare that I could finish a book; books I was told were great either bored the hell out of me or struck me as so sentimental and manipulative I wanted to throw them across the room. And writers, at least the male ones in Canada that I knew of (I was speaking about one former high school friend) were a bit dodgy as far as I was concerned, dickish because being a dick was somehow more authentic, convinced of their brilliance because they rarely lost a game of Trivial Pursuit.

When I told her, she reached across the table to take my hand in hers.

"You know that game, Trivial Pursuit?"

She nodded. "I have seen it. I know the word. I try not to be trivial."

She said she wasn't sure if she could find her way with the craft, but she had begun to write on a daily basis. Just her thoughts in a notebook. She had to start somewhere. "This is my summer to start things new, to start over."

At the time I imagined she meant starting over living in Canada, that she had regrets about arriving and working in Montreal. And because I knew that she and Petar had been lovers, I didn't want to pursue that line of conversation. The only lover I wanted her to think about was me.

I want to remember those few weeks we had that summer as nothing but idyllic. A lot of it was. We bought cheap second-hand bicycles from Igor, a local drug dealer and former Slovenian cop who flirted with Nataša and gave us a deal (later, I discovered the bikes were stolen). We explored the city on the weekends when Alex wasn't painting. In Alex's kitchen we made dinner for each other from what we could find in Kensington Market. She loved the grit and the energy of it down there on Saturdays. "So many punks and hippies, it's like the Sarajevo I remember before the war." She said Alex had gotten mad at her because her arms and legs had tanned so darkly but to me she was only more beautiful. Even the brown of her eyes seemed to darken in the summer light.

Yet there were days when she would become withdrawn, practically push me away. Some evenings after our dinner together she would get quiet, tell me she did not want anyone in her bed, that she preferred to be alone (she rarely slept at my place, I wonder now if it was because she had less control over her environment). She would not get angry with me so much as inexplicably withdrawn, with a bitter sarcasm in her voice if I tried to lighten her mood. On these occasions I could not help myself, I had to ask her if it was me, something I was doing to make her feel this way. If I knew what it was, I said, I could try to fix it. Perhaps she misheard me, the last time I tried this approach, but she became angry with me. She leaned into the table between us. "You can't fix me. How dare you! Don't you even fucking try." She tapped the candle flame out with her bare fingers and then ran upstairs to her room in Alex's house and locked the door. I should have realized then she was retracting from our intimacy, fitfully trying to end our relationship.

Still her resolve wavered—she would come back around, answer my phone calls with a warmth in her voice that made me feel that she regretted our time apart. She forgave my incursions on her solitude. I tried to be as detached and unsentimental as she was, but I was bad at caution, hopelessly uncool. I'd bring her flowers, she would kiss me and thank me, and then leave them wrapped in plastic in her kitchenette.

It was in the last two weeks of August that I felt a distance open up that I could not close again. It began when Petar came to visit Alex, ostensibly to work on a video installation in what Alex called his annex—a converted toolshed he used to store paintings. Petar had an effect on her; his presence made her sullen and withdrawn. By then I had been doing some part-time work for Alex, helping him with his website, his business correspondence, and the online catalogue of his work. Nataša had made this happen, I could tell; she knew I wanted to be a part of this world as much as I needed the money. I did not see anything happen between Petar and her, nothing to make me jealous anyway. Yet his mere presence in her life transformed her. She even started to question Alex's authenticity.

"You know Alex is obsessed about money. Isn't that vulgar? He has so much cash packed in a suitcase in his studio. He showed it to me."

I was hesitant to say anything negative about Alex. He had given me work, after all, based on nothing more than a conversation over dinner in his house and Nataša's kind words about my character and my ambition.

"I don't know. It's just like Alex to flaunt that, show he actually doesn't care about money at all."

"Flaunt. I like that word. He hasn't flaunted it to you though, has he?"

"No. That's true."

"It's sixty-four thousand dollars, Lucien. That's a lot to flaunt. And when I asked him about it he got all proud, he said that was the amount his first real painting sold for in New York. He calls it his fuck-off money."

"Maybe he's sentimental about that time in his life when he first broke out."

Nataša laughed. A welcome break in her cloud of melancholy, considering how she had been since Petar's arrival. "There is nothing sentimental about Alex. That is why we get along so well."

What she couldn't say: *and that's why I can't see a future for us, Lucien.*

I responded as best I could, giving her as much space in our silences for her to believe I was capable of her detachment. If her moods darkened, if she suddenly seemed consumed by bad memories and dark thoughts, I would not probe. And because I believed we were learning to love each other, I was determined to be as good a student as possible, given the limited curriculum provided.

About a week later, on one of those rare occasions when she had slept at my place, I was up early, working on Alex's website, going through his old slides, when she came up behind me and gently put her arms around my shoulders as we looked through the images together.

"You know why I like Alex's work, Lucien? When he showed me his old catalogues . . . you see he's always changing. He's tracing the history of painting, but with his own work he's never looking back. Only looking forward."

I nodded. But the truth was I didn't see Alex's work that way at all. All these slides confirmed how little his work had changed. It was as if there was an essential painting he was trying to produce, once he stripped away all other options and approaches. He was using painting to solve a mystery some central image presented. It heartened me, because I felt it was what I was trying to figure out with photography.

Now I think maybe there was something to be learned from Alex's solitude as well: don't try to solve anyone.

Anyway, I couldn't leave my response at a nod. "Do you think it's possible to be so remorseless about your own past?"

"Possible?" She smiled, one of the last times I saw that grin. "It's more than possible. It's necessary."

Two days later she finally broke up with me.

But of course, on the night of the blackout, the whole world changed. There was suddenly so much to solve about Alex's past, so much to finally learn about Nataša's.

5. Dejan Vidić

It all went wrong for me and Nataša the night the power went out in Toronto. It was supposed to be the night we put the second phase of the plan into action. Her plan. It was going to be simple: once that artist friend of hers was out for a night I would break in downstairs, steal the suitcase with the money. I would make it look like a burglary, a crackhead looking to take whatever was of value. But then the fucking guy came home, right in the middle of it. And the idiot got a knife in his kitchen and cornered me. What was supposed to be simple became very complicated.

It wasn't me who did it. We both slashed the paintings. She took the suitcase with the money—we'd split it when we met up again. But once I left, things went bad with the parking guy. I needed the Merc. That was unfortunate and an accident. I mean, you have the video. I am prepared for the trial and the decision. Anyway, Rebane, I tell you, Rebane was all her, not me.

My jealousy. My jealousy and my idiot passion. Everybody warned me when I was younger. My first girlfriend back home, back before the war, Ana, said "Dejan, one day you're going to get into a fight there will be only one way to finish. You want that?' But you know, after the army, I changed, okay? You come to love your own freedom because you realize everyone is trying to take it away from you.

What can I tell you, I loved her. From the first moment I saw Nataša, when she walked into the Swan back in London. There was that moment of recognition. She took away my freedom. I knew, given the chance, I would do anything it took. What that meant, I never could have imagined. Nataša.

You have to understand what her first email from Canada did to me. I was sure she had forgotten I existed. She had gone to Canada to be with Petar. I had lost her to him. It was hard to accept, but I got it. He had money. He said he had a career as an artist. I have no illusions. I worked the door at the Swan. I'm nobody's first choice. But as soon as I saw she had written me, I wasn't going to let her get away from me.

She didn't say much in those first messages. But then she sent an old video clip that she had found, going through files Petar had. It was from our army days. I could tell, as soon as I saw the blurry image of the patch of forest, that it was Foča. Fucking Petar, was my first thought. Why did he have to go and find this? Him and his art nonsense. All she asked me in that message was to view the clip and to call her. She gave me her new Canadian number.

I was prepared for the worst with the call. I immediately tried to apologize. I told her I did not mean to deceive her because I never mentioned I was involved with Foča. You have to understand, I did not know about her father. And the clip, well . . . I know what it means for me. But she stopped me before I could go on, make it worse for myself. She forgave me. She knew I was a kid, in the middle of something I had no control over, I was trying to survive.

And then she posed the question: "Dejan, how much money do you think you would need to start your life over, a whole new person?" It caught me off balance. A million? It was the first number in my head. "So that's about two million for two people then." I still didn't know where she was going with this. "If I asked you to come to Canada for me, what would you say?"

And that's how it began.

Not long after, she sent out the video clip to Petar, Nikola, and me, demanding the money. I had been in Canada about a week at that point, living in a motel in the east end of Toronto. With the gypsies and the fucking Africans. Not my idea of a vacation. I was doing what she instructed: waiting. Laying low, as she called it. Six straight nights of Big Macs, nothing on the TV but baseball. I'm sorry, it's a stupid game. When I called her all she said was that we had to be patient, that we could finally be together when Alex left his house for more than an hour.

I swore to her I would go along with the plan with the video. I'd ensure we got the money from Petar and Nikola. It was all going to work out for her and me. If I had been in my right mind, if anyone else would have asked me to do what she was asking, I would have said no thanks, I'm out. The illusion of complete freedom, yes? You chase it like a greyhound with a fake fucking rabbit.

About the parking attendant, I'm happy to give you a confession. It's all there on video, nothing to hide. It's simple, after it was all over with Rebane she and I knew we had to split up, get invisible fast. And I wasn't going to manage that if I didn't get some wheels.

I know how to do this. Back home after the war, the best job I ever had was working for Nenad Zutić, he had us jacking Mercs and Beemers in Moscow then driving them all the way home on Polish plates. It's like second nature for me now. And in these lots, when they give these attendants the goddamn keys, they make it that much easier.

I didn't expect this guy Malik would resist. I mean, why? The Merc wasn't his car. It made no sense, but he left me no choice. I had a knife from Rebane's kitchen on me. Here's my advice: don't ever take a knife with you on the street unless you're prepared to use it, and you're prepared for the consequences. I suppose I was. I wasn't prepared for what happened with Rebane, as I said. And I swear to you, even though now it kills me to say it, Nataša was. It's like she was prepared for everything.

6. Christina Perretti

The one thing I've learned after twelve years is that for all the talk in a detective's training about the rational, orderly process of deduction, this work is far more creative and intuitive. It's at moments of crisis that you get the breakthroughs.

That's what Alex Rebane's death was. When I got the word back in my office in Milan, it was as though all the information we had been amassing in the art crimes unit, the narrative I had begun to piece together on an international forgery ring, had suddenly been destroyed. The murder was like fragments of a jigsaw puzzle scattering. There was nothing left to do but fly over there, work with the Toronto police and slowly put the whole story back together again.

Not that the police had much to start with. Rebane's murder had occurred on the night of a huge blackout that blanketed Toronto and a good portion of the northeastern United States in darkness for hours. All they had at the time were two homicides about a thousand metres apart downtown: Rebane and a parking attendant, Imad Malik. And Nataša Ružić had gone missing, but at that stage they were sure she'd be found in less than twenty-four hours. She was a prime suspect.

As for the homicides, there was trauma from stab wounds on both victims, but it was too early for the police to confirm whether the same blade had been used. The possibility that there would be anyone who knew both victims was remote at best.

When I arrived, I knew I couldn't come on too strong. Beat cops are the same in every city; I have to play the humble bureaucrat from Interpol, half tourist, half trainee. And the Toronto police responded in kind—solicitous, patronizing in the most charming way possible. They told me they were looking into Rebane's closest professional contacts: "item one," they had his book of contacts. A younger detective, this guy Aquino, pulled me aside to inform me that nine times out of ten the victim knows his murderer. He and another, older officer were going through the numbers in Rebane's phone. They were optimistic, but I had my doubts.

Rebane was not the main focus of what we were investigating in art crimes. He was an associate of Georg Barany, a suspected art forger I had been looking into for about six months. But whatever had happened, I just knew it was connected to what we were uncovering. There was too much money involved, and too many people who would benefit from what Rebane had to offer.

So I got on a plane, with a promise to my boss in Rome that I would only be a few days. I didn't expect much to come of it. "With this one, don't make any promises you can't keep," he said.

As usual, he was right. There was still so much to learn.

7. Lucien Bollinger

It was the morning after the blackout—August fifteenth of last year. I was lying on the floor when I heard my phone ring. On cue, the ceiling light flickered then brightened with a surge. I opened my eyes to see the blades of the old ceiling fan begin to turn once again.

I let the phone ring then hauled myself off the floor where I had laid out my futon close to the front window. The stark little warehouse space was a ghost of a home I could not really afford. I hadn't slept well because sirens had wailed all night through the Parkdale streets. And yet if I had closed the window, I would have been gasping for air and sweating through the vivid dreams brought on by too much wine. I was still hurting from the split with Nataša. To be fully awake at that moment asked too much of me.

As I shuffled down the hall to the bathroom, the phone rang again. No one ever calls me that early, not even my mother, regardless of how urgent things with my father might be. And this was the second time since, what, 8:30? This time nothing more than curiosity had me heading back to the kitchen to pick up.

I cleared my throat, answered in work tone. The voice on the other end of the line introduced himself: Detective Aquino from 52 Division.

Alex was dead and Nataša had disappeared.

Aquino needed me to come down to 52 Division, said he'd like to have "a short chat." My name and number were on Alex's phone, they were interviewing everyone in Alex's circle of friends. I wasn't sure if I was a friend of Alex's, I wanted to say. I'm not sure if anyone really knew him. I told him I had done some odd jobs for him and my ex-girlfriend was staying at his house. I didn't know how much I could help, but yes, I would be at 52 Division as soon as I could.

I stood there for about a minute after Aquino hung up. I could hear the hum of the air conditioner in the other room, working again. I stared out at the street through the dusty slats of the blinds. There was a neighbourhood regular in his dreadlocks and snowy beard, stretching his legs and mumbling by the entrance to the parkette across the street, squinting in the brassy morning light. The blackout had done wonders to lessen the wild energy around my corner. The crackheads and street dealers had retreated to cooler, darker places. Then I realized, if Alex was dead from a botched burglary, Nataša might have been attacked as well, her room was right above Alex's.

Surely she would have called, left a message, told me something, anything about what had gone on. *Just let her be okay.* I hurried across the room to where my phone was charging. Not one call. I scrolled through the names and numbers. Yes, I'd called Alex a couple of times over the last few days, arranging a time I could go to his place, for work. And of course I'd called Nataša two days before, but that was just to meet for dinner and a walk through Trinity Bellwoods Park. My poor man's attempts at romance before she told me she didn't want to see me anymore. Anyway, she had not called overnight and, what was worse, when I tried her now, her number was out of service.

Nataša can no longer be reached, and Alex Rebane is dead. Putting those two facts together in my mind implied a connection I couldn't accommodate.

My thoughts went to another scenario that did not cause me to question everything I knew about Nataša. She must have found Alex Rebane and then fled, in fear for her life.

I slumped on the floor, my back propped against the torn leather couch. I held my throbbing, wine-heavy head in my hands. My fingers prickled, raw from all the nicotine still coursing through me. I had to quit smoking, yet if I ever needed a cigarette it was at that moment.

I figured Nataša must be wandering the streets. I had a feeling, from the way she had talked about immigrating, that her visitor's visa was expired. Maybe she had bolted at the sight of the police downstairs, scared she'd be questioned, suspected. That was just like her—fear of any kind of authority.

Maybe she was making her way over to see me without her phone. She could have realized our relationship was the one thing in her life that might be good for her. Listen to me, my arrogance. To my mind there was no reason for her to have ended our relationship, we both knew we had strong feelings for each other. She had fought my appeals. Love, she said, like hate, really wasn't rational, and at the very least I couldn't expect such thinking from her. And now this.

In my taxi to the police station, the speed and the sense of movement were soothing. It was progress. I was closer to more information and it was easier to be hopeful, to imagine that this morning, serious as it was, was not about to change my life. I had gotten myself together. I was ready for the worst of it.

Aquino, the one I had spoken to on the phone, met me at the reception, took me upstairs to the end of the hall, and threw open a door like we were raiding the place. With the blinds up, the morning light blazed from the bank of windows on the other side of an interview room. The glare turned Aquino and his partner into blurry grey outlines of shoulders, thick necks, and thatched heads, slumped and bearing down for the questions ahead.

Aquino introduced me to his partner, Detective Fortune, and we exchanged nods and the briefest of grins. If Detective Aquino was the young and ambitious kid who worked by the book, Fortune looked like the institutional memory in the room. He had the lined and weathered face of an old barfly. I was sizing them up, making snap judgments, presuming they hadn't already sized me up and determined I was inconsequential, a bit player in what was going on.

Aquino introduced me to the woman seated behind them, taking notes: Detective Perretti, from Interpol in Milan. It dawned on me that Alex's death would be of international interest because of his history and the profile he once had in the art world. Perretti said her hello with two distinct, measured syllables. She had the husky voice of a heavy smoker.

Aquino ruffled the papers in front of him and stuck a pencil behind his ear. He smiled for me, and demanded I tell them about my relationship with Alex Rebane.

His tone was aggressive. I felt like he was performing for Perretti and Fortune, to reassure them he was in control. Napoleon complex. So maybe I got a little defensive in turn, clearing up any misconceptions to start. No, I wasn't Alex Rebane's lover and no, I wasn't his drug dealer, didn't touch the stuff. As far as I knew, Alex had cleaned up. It was as much a shock to me as it was to everyone.

With that, Fortune took two photographs of Alex's bludgeoned corpse out of a grey envelope. He spoke so quietly, I could barely hear him over the air conditioning. "This is how Alex Rebane died, Mr. Bollinger."

I glanced at the odd, rag-doll positioning of Alex's body on his

Afghan carpet, the blue patches in the rug turned purple from the blood. I felt like I was going to vomit and put my hand over my mouth. But I kept my composure and managed to get a question out: If this was how Alex had died, where was Nataša?

With that Perretti moved in closer to listen. She looked concerned for me. It did not make me feel any better.

Aquino pulled back, shot a quick look over at Fortune, who nodded. "So you were seeing Nataša Ružić, the tenant who is missing?"

I nodded. For a few weeks over the summer I had liked to think of her as my girlfriend, I said. Fortune and Aquino briefly looked to each other and with one nod, on cue, leaned forward.

"Well, let's talk about her, if we can," Aquino said.

And so I told them what I thought they would need to know. The first time we met, when she had come to my English as a second language class, the weeks of dating that stretched into the summer, the moment I suddenly realized she and I might actually be in a relationship. And then her breaking it off with me little more than a couple of days before.

Fortune was frowning at the notes he had started to make in a notebook in front of him. "You can understand that all of this about her is a little puzzling. She was supposed to be working in a gallery in Montreal. That's on her work visa. That she was living at Rebane's and . . . all this."

"*Was* living?"

"She's now a missing person, Mr. Bollinger."

I was irritated by all three of them now. What were they doing here, casually interviewing me? Alex had been murdered, and Nataša could have been abducted. Who knew what kind of cruelty she could be suffering, given what I had seen of Alex's body? But I stayed calm, sighed as I exhaled. Perretti wouldn't take her eyes off me, and it took all I had not to challenge her. I told them

Nataša had come to Toronto for the summer, that she was modelling for a series of paintings Alex was working on, in an arrange-
ment with her employer, Caroline Vidler, of the Vidler Gallery
in Montreal.

"I want you to take a look at one of these photographs again,
Mr. Bollinger," said Aquino. He handed it to me and I could feel
myself blush, embarrassed by the intimacy of the murder scene in
my hands. "Look over in the top left. You see a briefcase there?
Got any idea what might have been in it?"

I shook my head, with a little too much certainty. Why did I
feel I had to perform my innocence? "Not a clue."

After an awkward pause, Fortune cleared his throat and fingered a photocopied news clipping in front of him. "I'm not sure
if you're aware of this, but Alex Rebane exhibited his work at the
Casale Gallery earlier this year."

"I was there, yes."

"So we've done a little work here. There were two paintings
that caused quite a shitstorm, I'd say: one called *Salome's Revenge*
and the other *The Spirit of Liberty*. In both there's a woman—I
guess this is Nataša Ružić—in a headscarf and not much else."

"That's right." I nodded and blinked. I knew where he was
taking this, and I was going to perform being unfazed.

"So in one of these there's like painted verses from the Ko-
ran in graffiti on a kind of bullet-scarred wall behind her image,
right?"

"I know of them."

"Okay so there's this Amit Chaudhury—a cleric in London—
you know what he said about that one? He said he saw no difference between what Rebane did and what that guy did with that
novel . . . That he deserved to be judged for it. It's right here in the
Globe." Fortune stabbed his thumb on the newspaper in front of
him. Thick, butcher's hands. His knuckles were scarred.

"I did read that, yes. The guy's a nutjob."

Fortune slid another envelope across the table to me. I reached in and fingered the first few photographs, gently sliding them out. There was a shot of blood smeared along two canvases. I felt the nausea rise in my throat again.

"The first seven are strictly of the paintings," Aquino said. "You may want to avoid the rest."

Whoever had killed Alex had taken a blade to each canvas, gouged out the eyes of the subject, slashed at the faces beyond recognition. Flipping through the photos, I saw this particular violence had been carried out on all six he was working on.

"Tell me, Mr. Bollinger—" It was all Fortune could do not to shoot a wink at Aquino as he spoke. "Now I know fuck all about art, but is that normal? I don't mean what's been done to these paintings. I mean that's obviously psycho. I'm talking about the way Rebane worked. Six at once, all in different states of completion."

I was puzzled more than anything. It all seemed beside the point. I think I said something about Alex painting in a hurry. He felt he had a lot of time to make up for from his years of addiction. He had told me this himself, I knew I was on safe ground.

Perretti nodded. I had a feeling my answer had met her approval in some way.

And so I kept on talking, saying that I knew he didn't have much time with Nataša, either. She had promised Caroline Vidler and her partner Petar that she would return to Montreal at the end of August.

Perretti of all three looked the most interested in what I had to say about Caroline and Petar. So why not be of help, I figured. Anything if it got them working to find Nataša. I pulled out my wallet from my back pocket and flipped through the plastic cards until I found what I was looking for. "Petar Stepanović, there you go." I passed it over to Aquino, who nodded as he shared it with Fortune and Perretti. "All I know is he and Caroline Vidler have a small gallery in the old part of the city, though my sense is she runs it. He tries to be some kind of artist. Video or something. Anyway, Petar and Nataša. Though they're both from Sarajevo, they actually met in London. At least that's what she told me. He was there for his work and she was living there with friends. They hit it off."

"And you met Stepanović in Montreal?" Fortune was eyeing the card carefully. He seemed to find something objectionable about the card's design.

"No, here in Toronto. He had come for Alex's last show. They were friends. Alex told me Caroline Vidler gave him a show when no one else would."

"You think Nataša's headed back to Montreal?"

"I'd say more than likely. I'm sure you know Nataša's cell's been disconnected."

"Yes," Aquino said quietly, nodding. "First thing we checked in her room. The phone is gone."

"I called Petar myself."

"But you didn't get a hold of him."

"No, but that's not unusual. He keeps his voicemail box full and screens his calls. He doesn't want to talk to me."

"And why's that?"

"Probably because he thinks Nataša would be better off without me. He and Caroline, they seemed protective of her, like she was their project."

"You think he's got something to hide?"

I smiled. I was remembering walking up Ossington with Nataša on a rainy night, three, four weeks before. We had left Café Saigon and she had said yes to another drink. She was opening up to me at last. "Petar's got a lot of secrets, Lucien. Like any interesting person." Maybe I should have told Fortune and Aquino about that, but I mumbled that I had no idea.

Aquino looked to Fortune, who nodded as he handed him Petar Stepanović's black business card. Aquino did not even look back at me as he bolted from the room.

I tried to make light of Aquino's dramatic exit, and it riled Perretti enough that she had to respond. "He's in a hurry because he knows of your friend," she said.

It was clear from Fortune's face that she had spoken out of turn. She wouldn't even look his way. She leaned back in her chair once again, and with a prim snap of a small buckle on her notebook, she was done.

"In your work for Alex Rebane . . ." Fortune ruffled his papers in front of him, squinting down the page. He seemed to have lost his thought.

"Odd jobs, clerical. I mean, I hardly knew him."

Fortune looked up from his page. He found my tone of interest. I guess I would have thought the same.

"In your time at his house, did he ever talk to you of threats he had received?"

"What kind of threats?"

"I'm talking people from the Muslim community who might have been angry with him. The way he painted Nataša."

I shook my head. I'm sure I looked incredulous.

"Mr. Bollinger, you're not going anywhere for the next few days, are you? I mean out of the city?"

"Is that a question or an order, Detective Fortune?"

"Depends on your answer."

"I can be here if you need me for further questioning."

"There you go. Thank you, sir."

I rose and nodded. "You're welcome." I could sense Perretti taking me in, her arms folded, so unconvinced of my innocence.

In the hall, my eyes adjusted to the fluorescent light. It was as if someone had turned down the volume on the morning. The grey broadloom, the officers mumbling a few metres ahead. There was a softened and blurry edge to everything. I followed Fortune as the detective strutted down the hall, shoulders pinned back. I felt a wave of nausea gather and lift, threatening to break my composure as I thought of those photographs again, but I swallowed deeply and blinked away the dark spots that suddenly appeared in front of my eyes. I felt so frail, it was all I could do to focus on an image of my futon splayed out on the floor, the tangled sheets waiting for me.

"I've always liked painting, going to art galleries. It's interesting, isn't it?"

If this was Fortune's attempt at detective work, pitching a goofy and obtuse line out there to see if I swung and connected with some damning response, then he was dumber than he looked. But I played along, asked him why he thought painting was interesting.

"I guess because there's a little crazy in it. The good stuff, I'm talking about. It's good crazy, not bad crazy."

"I guess you see enough bad crazy on the job, eh?"

He opened the last of the glass doors along the hall, shrugged and heaved out a breathy sigh. If he was frustrated by my turning the tables and asking the questions, he was not going to show it.

"You don't know the half of it, my friend. So, to be clear, you're going to stick around and be available if we need you back."

"I'll make sure of it."

As I pushed open the door, wincing from the blast of heat, I squinted back at Fortune, still on the air-conditioned side of the conversation. I needed to show him I would look him in the eye, that all the grief, confusion, and sadness in me was real. It wasn't about disabusing Fortune of any notion I was guilty; it was simpler than that. There was an urgent need: *find Nataša and save her.* Because I could not do it on my own. I took in Fortune's nod and feeble wave then turned to find myself a cab.

8. Nataša Ružić: Notebook One

This little notebook is all I have now. Well, aside from tired feet, sore knees and a burn on the side of my face from just one hour of this morning sun. Sleeping rough, as they would say back there in Hackney (that seems a century ago now). I used to write down expressions like that in here, but I ripped out those pages when I came to Canada. It seems I always have to begin again. A fresh start, a new pen, maybe a new me. Once I get the old me down here.

"Put one word after another." That is what Lucien told me when I said that I wanted to write but I found it so hard. Well, I'm finally taking his words to heart. I think of him reaching across the café table in that doughnut shop near the bus station in his neighbourhood. "Your story is as important as anybody else's, and I think memory is who we are." I'd prefer to think of it as who we used to be. I am saying goodbye to that person and Lucien will have to say goodbye to her too, I'm afraid.

Apart from this notebook and of course the money—more money than I've ever seen—I also have a video camera from Alex's house. But I don't consider it mine now, and I still don't really know how to work it. An ugly, hungry eye wrapped in black plastic, it fits in my hand as if it were a ball of light I must carry through the dark. I look through the eyepiece and see an outline of a square and a blur, a flashing light that no button I can press seems to stop. I have got some time to try and figure this out and I suppose I should, to tape myself, confirm I am alive. I would prefer not to put my face in front of a camera, though. What good has a camera ever done me? If that English word on the side of this one—focus—means anything, I take it as a sign I should be writing, not feeding someone else's eyes.

I know, focus is just a word on the side of a lens, but I do look for signs everywhere. Most of the time, when I read a sign, it turns out to be right.

For example, there's an old guy with big striped shorts and baseball cap, over there on the sand with his metal detector. He looks a bit like Mussolini, so I'm going to call him Benito. If Benito finds something while I write this, it's a sign this beach is safe, and I can sleep here again tonight. If Benito finds nothing, it's a sign I should move on. I know, some people might read this in the opposite way, but I believe you have to trust how the sign comes to you, the rules it imposes.

Is that crazy? Probably. I'm not going to say that everything in here is going to make sense. "The writer must play God," my uncle-who-was-never-my-uncle Milan told me years ago in my other life (call it Nataša part one). Once God makes sense, so will I, how's that?

Still, if I were to claim God-like powers, if even for a moment, I would say I outdid myself with my email, sent to Mr. Nikola Lazarević of Vancouver, Canada, Petar, and my poor, foolish Dejan, who actually seems to have feelings for me:

Gentlemen,

Please find attached a video clip which might be of interest to you. This is of an incident in a village called Foča not so long ago, where the three of you can be identified carrying out a war crime. Petar, I have you to thank for this clip.

I would be happy to provide the ICC in the Hague with this evidence.
There is only one course of action for you that will prevent this. $2 million
US will buy my silence and the destruction of the original of this tape.

Account details forthcoming. I look forward to hearing from you.

Justice is mine and I will repay, says the Lord. Well, there it is. I worked on the wording for at least an hour, I've got three versions in the back pages of this notebook. But as soon as I pressed send those few days ago (though it seems like so much longer now), I realized there is no turning back. I will take this to the very end.

This is not a suicide note. If it is a goodbye, it is only addressed to the young woman I used to be, little Nataša. All her names: the Quiet One, the Most Promising, the Troublemaker, the Bad Influence, the Actress. I imagine all these various episodes, locked away in a camera like this one. I took on these roles, but now they are reams of footage you could hack away from the film of my life, and what would be left would be the sequences of a woman running. Running for cover. When I get to the last word on the last page here, only then will I catch my breath.

I'm looking forward to the moment I can write it. But there's a lot to get down in a hurry, I suppose. And there's still some distance to run.

If I could write anything to Lucien now it would be this. Please don't think the worst of me. You were chasing a woman who did not mean to deceive you. From moment to moment the Nataša I had been tried to live truthfully. It was the only way I could try to be good. As if truth and goodness have ever been more than passing acquaintances, I know.

The morning is bright and sunny on the beach of this lake where no one swims. On a clear day you can look out and see, across those waves like the Miljačka's, a shoreline in America— though I don't know where on a map it would be. Right now, in the first hour of full light, it is kind of beautiful and peaceful. Pine trees on a beach there, all the branches bent to mime the force of the wind. It's how I know here could only be Canada. I know I'm going to have to be vigilant about stealing these moments whenever I can right now, until all of this is over.

Though it is still me and Benito over there. A little earlier a woman, small and slim, all tight little muscles in her running singlet and shorts, she went running by and gave me a look like I was some human garbage on the beach. Maybe because of my backpack and the state of these boots. Well, what do you want from me? I walked through what seemed like a swamp in the night, okay? If I had been able to see more than a few centimetres in front of me, maybe I would be more presentable to all you oh-so-proper Canadians. Women like her used to make me angry, now they make me tired.

Like Caroline Vidler. But I am ahead of myself. She is for the Nataša part two of my writing.

There is only one thing I must do, now that the worst has happened. I have to get to my uncle Milan. Only he can help me with the lawyers and the translators to shoot my way free of the Alex situation. He's also my insurance to finally sever ties with Dejan if it comes to that, given who he knows in the government back home. But easier said than done, right? I look at the map, and this country is ridiculous. Getting to Vancouver is going to be like crossing Russia on foot. I have no choice. With everything that's happened now, I am making my way like a homeless person, unnoticed, a figure in the background no one can remember enough to describe.

Everywhere it seems, once you begin to look for them, you see cameras. Cameras at the entrances of nightclubs and bars, cameras in every bank where those who have no home go to sleep by the ATMs. I'm getting some idea now of how difficult it is to stay invisible.

I must try to find shelter and a place to sleep. With all the lights out last night I wonder what images were captured on that videotape. Shadows moving through the heat and the grey fog, perhaps. Ghost figures. That is what I'm going to become. If I can't disappear myself under the gaze of these cameras, I can at least become a ghost. I know I can't do anything about the photos and videos taken of me, but I wish they could all be destroyed.

I look up from my notebook. Benito has placed his metal detector on the sand and he is crouching a few feet from where the waves unfurl and lap the shore. This is my moment of decision: value or unvalue (is that a word? it should be). He's got powerful legs for an older man. Maybe he played football? Something tells me he wasn't born in this country, a feeling I got from his measured, elegant way of walking. He seems a man used to different kinds of streets, a place presented on the scale of the walking person, not someone who takes in the world from a car window or the view from a surveillance camera. His shorts and shirt look pressed. He seems to have more vanity than these Canadians, who have no shame about the way their bellies hang outside their T-shirts. He has examined a piece of glass that looks from here to have had a gold rim along one edge. A broken tumbler, tossed off the side of a pleasure boat long ago, perhaps. He flings it into the water with a flick of his wrist. Unvalue.

So it is settled, then: I must move on. And that is just as well. How to figure out leaving the city, knowing I am sure to be traced once I step into a bank or a bus station, these are the problems to solve right now. I have nothing but time to put my mind to them, I suppose. At least for now. Focus, as the camera says, and, like the good Nataša I once was, I will obey.

9. Milan Zujović

I remember the day Nataša first emailed me, welcoming me to Canada. She was so strangely enthusiastic. It was the day of my first rehearsal in Vancouver of *The Blood of Agamemnon*. We were scheduled to begin at 8:30 in the morning, and given the time change from Chicago, where I had been living for a few months, it was much too early for me to be lucid, never mind say anything of value about the remount. Nataša's message, calling me "Uncle Milan" for the first time in two years, was enough to put me off balance. It gave me a strange feeling about the play.

Which was justified, I suppose, all things considered. How to grieve, how to rebuild a life—that is something the play never deals with. I don't know how many times I've sat in press conferences or across the table from some journalist and spoken about art's ability to heal our pain. My art feels completely useless to me now.

As soon as I arrived in the city, I was already finding it hard to connect my original feelings and images for the play with the touring spectacle it had become. I can remember going through the main doors of the theatre lobby that morning. I could hear the hum of a vacuum cleaner, from somewhere up on the second floor leading to the balconies. These theatres all look the same in the west; they're big barns, fake-regal, and vaguely religious, like theme park cathedrals.

The first remarks by the director to the actors must be endured, I know. Hanno Borschmann, the former artistic director in Lille, once told me we must be ambassadors of art—for our actors as much as for our audiences. The same Hanno Borschmann who, around the time the Baader Meinhof Gang was imprisoned, had staged the *Winterreise* in an abattoir and considered speaking about any work of his as an act of imperialistic aggression on the imagination. I wonder what he'd think of that now. The mind's been colonized by so much, so many images wash over us. The imagination has long been an occupied country, comrade. Our little chats for our actors prior to the work ahead barely register, as I'm sure he'd agree.

The theatre was empty, save for the few actors in row C and two men on the tech crew, arms folded in their laps. They were laden with devices; there were army knives, light meters and keys clipped onto their belt loops, as if they were prepared for an expedition or a military operation. I made my way to the stage where two card tables had been placed together side by side, along with three chairs. I was all set to perform when an image of Nataša as a young production assistant flashed before me. I could see her out there among the journalists, snapping her gum, examining her fingernails, blowing her bangs off her forehead with a pouty bottom lip, bored once again.

Let me say I am very excited and honoured to be working with you here on the challenging work of Mister Aleksei Golimov.

I can do all this posturing, but it is not my forte. These codes of conduct were all but unknown to me for decades, when I was— let's be honest—an obscure, not-quite-radical director, staging Beckett and Ionesco in small university towns in Europe, all the while hoping that some teaching post for a semester or two would turn into a permanent position, and that I would be saved from going from one joyless act of theatrical commemoration to another.

I would be dead now if that were still my life. I never would have had the strength to give up drinking.

But back to the room: there I was, compelled once again to perform for actors. I tapped my foot, all nerves below the table. I apologized for being a little late. Success—whatever that might mean on this scale—has done very little to fortify the brick-by-brick construction of the platitudes that keep self-doubt at bay. Radical, uncompromising, visionary—all the adjectives that have been attached to my name for marketing purposes are now irrelevant. How about dependable, co-operative and reliable? Being a little late, a little unkempt, and a little outspoken is all a part of the conventional product I deliver now, on budget and, for the time being, immune to commercial failure. I make reliable, quality entertainment dressed up as something of greater substance. As Mira told me in one of my moments of despair after the Chicago previews, "Do you know how few of you there are? You'll always have work now."

Yet I had nothing profound to say as I took the initial questions from the actors. The only way to explain the world of the play was to talk about war mind. It was an expression I coined in rehearsals for the way all the characters reacted to one another. I was arguing with Mira, who has been playing Clytemnestra for three years—my wife was my choice for the role from the very beginning. She was having difficulty with a particular scene, and I told her she had to realize that all these characters reacted to each other out of this state of being: a kind of animal fear that blocks out better thinking. That's all I should have said about it, but no, I had to talk politics.

Specifically, I had to talk about what had occurred when I was working on *The Blood of Agamemnon* in Chicago. Our first week in rehearsals coincided with the invasion of Iraq. Maybe it was different up here, but all the papers, after one week, declared a victory. That, I said, was typical war mind in its denial. It was like Clytemnestra in this tragedy, a bit too quick to claim victory. She seeks revenge, she gets it. Mission accomplished!

I went on, talking about Cassandra as a crazy street girl. She's the one who is immune to the denial of war mind. She can see more carnage coming, a curse on the house. More blood for blood.

Perhaps it was just a delayed reaction about America. I was finally processing what I had witnessed down there. I needed to make an argument for political intentions in art to these mild-mannered Canadians. I was refuting what I had heard from Mira and other wise voices about how any polemical gesture reduces the power of a work, narrows its range of meaning and makes it topical. I don't think Golimov, God rest his soul, wanted this work to be . . . blanched, can I say? Bleached, bleached of its political impact. His plays were banned for close to twenty years. Like Shostakovich, he went through hell. He did not have time to conceal his motives.

I said that when I read any work for the first time, I ask myself a simple question: why must this be on stage? You have to credit my honesty. Just don't confuse it with integrity. First you ask yourself about action, what must take place. Then you ask yourself the tougher question: why. Why is some action shown, and why is some action not shown?

You see, I really do believe it: Golimov realized something about the Greeks and their drama, something that was only too real for him and his audience. A good play was about what you don't see rather than what you see, and all the real bloody business in the play, it is concealed. Out of the scene. Murder as obscenity.

The four actors were smiling uneasily, rigid in their seats. I had the feeling I was being humoured, indulged. I was the eccentric who had gotten a touch carried away and couldn't bring the first rehearsal back to the kind of conversation where we could all comfortably get down to work.

I couldn't leave things at what I know from experience. I had to pontificate on how we experience the mediated world, how we like to believe we have the full perspective. Nothing escapes our line of vision. We go from screen to screen. Computers—these devices . . . We experience so much of our world at a remove.

I really don't regret saying all this, though. I know it is true. Even in rehearsals, I look out at the crew, and no one is actually watching the performance. They're watching what is on their screens. Bear with me as I pontificate further and say we've been seduced into believing we can master time this way. It is the illusion of immediacy. We think we can live entirely in the present tense. Inside time, outside consequence.

As we got close to the end of that first session, I pictured Nataša in that audience once more. She was suddenly a ghost in the room. And that stopped me, much to everyone's relief.

Let me say that even now, after all that has happened, I will not believe in ghosts. I believe in stubborn, restless memories. It's all we have. Here is my confession about my work, if you want one. I don't believe I have any imagination, no ability to conjure up original images in my head. My so-called visionary work on stage consists of nothing but failed depictions of who and what still haunts me.

Of course Nataša does, when I close my eyes.

10. Lucien Bollinger

I knew I had to find Nataša, and, judging from all I had heard from the police, that meant getting to Montreal. I called Petar Stepanović, but just as he must have told the police, he said that he and Caroline had not had any contact with Nataša. Caroline was grieving over Alex and did not want to be disturbed, Petar said, as if it was a script he'd memorized. They would be in Toronto for Alex's funeral in a couple of days so why didn't we talk more then. I had no way of determining whether any of it was sincere. All I really had was the silence from the police and Nataša herself to ruminate over. I decided at some point over those forty-eight hours that followed her disappearance, that I was the only one who loved her and cared enough about her fate to take action. Yes, loved her.

Maybe one should never make these kinds of decisions when one feels powerless and alone. It is easier to believe in the idea of love rather than to truly love another, and I am someone who has difficulty distinguishing between those two states of being. Still, I decided action over reflection was required.

I needed to get a car so I could look for Nataša effectively or at the very least get to her quickly, as soon as I heard of her where-abouts. It could be a matter of life and death, I reasoned, because she would probably contact me rather than the police. I would take as much time off from teaching as I needed to. It was the only way I would feel that I wasn't languishing or doing less than I could to save her. My best option, given that I wasn't sure when or for how long I would need a vehicle, was to take a bus out to Milton, where my mother was living and where my father was in a care facility, and borrow their car.

There was a degree of low-level humiliation, coupled with a feeling of powerlessness at my father's situation, that I would have to deal with taking this journey. The humiliation was in the act of asking my aging, barely mobile mother for a loan of one of the few possessions she still had. It was true that she hardly ever drove that old Buick Regal anymore, she was too nervous about her failing eyesight and her nerves behind the wheel. Here I was, a man into my thirties now, living like a student, still not settled after returning from Tokyo more than a year before, with my father's dementia worsening by the day. Both he and my mother required the kind of care and attention real adults could provide. My older brother Henrik, the responsible one, settled with his wife and two boys in Oakville, was paying for a good portion of my father's stay at his facility and most of my mother's living expenses. I had yet to contribute anything, even though I had some money saved from my time in Tokyo untouched in the bank (my back-to-Tokyo emergency fund, I called it). "Save it for now, you might need it," Henrik had cautioned me at Christmas back in Milton, and I did not know how to take it as anything but the coldest dismissal of my prospects for ever providing for anyone. My mother nodded in agreement across the dinner table, and I suddenly had the feeling that for years, while I was away in Japan, I had been a topic of conversation at family functions, a problem that was probably never going to be solved. And now here I was returning to Milton, confirming the worst of what my mother had been led to expect.

In my mind there was bravery, maybe even something noble behind what to everyone else would seem foolhardy adventurism. I realized, as the bus to Milton pulled out of Union Station, that this was a common enough refrain in my head. I would not mention Rebane's death, would not explain to my mother or father the grave circumstances behind my borrowing the car, just as I never truly explained the real reason I went off to Japan for the first time, all those many years ago. It was as though I imagined that all would be revealed at the time of my death or something, when my diary was found. "The Japanese seem reserved on the surface, but inside we are practically hysterics," Keiko had once said to me. No wonder I fit in so well there. I liked to keep my drama to myself.

My time in Japan was the best case in point. I had told my family that my reason for travelling there was that I could pay off my student loans by getting a well-paying teaching job. I hoped to travel the world, figure out whether I would go on to further studies and become something like a sensible adult. It had seemed to them like the first wise decision I had made, apart from going to university in the first place (Henrik had gone to that same university before me and had studied engineering, and look what a success he was!). My secret motive was hidden in the tackle bag I slung around my shoulder and took everywhere. The old Compax camera my father had given to me in my first year of university. It was the only gift that I ever felt was truly from him. What I really wanted to do was figure out how to be an artist, how to capture something authentic about the world.

My love for the camera, and my belief that I might actually be talented at photography, began in university in London—that's London, Ontario, of course. The friends I had made were, like me, ill fitted for the ersatz Ivy League atmosphere. We made it a point of pride to own no tennis shirts, deck shoes, or ski sweaters, to steer clear of the pubs where the students would gather after varsity football and hockey games. No, we haunted the few music clubs where Toronto bands played to small but devoted crowds of ex-punks and goth kids with fake IDs.

We had perpetuated the code of musical tribes established in high school. The Toronto we hoped to move to after graduation was defined by the stretch of Queen Street that began at the Horseshoe Tavern at Spadina and headed west as far as Parkdale, where former suburban kids like me hoped to find a toehold in some kind of artistic community. I was hopeless as a musician: I could barely manage three chords on an acoustic guitar.

Where I discovered something of a talent was in photographing four friends of mine who had formed a band. I began shooting interiors of abandoned, faintly menacing industrial landscapes for the posters the group would put up around town, and soon I was shooting photos for other bands and getting my work in the *Gazette*, the student newspaper. I was dabbling in this just enough to ensure my grades didn't slip, so I could still plausibly claim to be keeping my options open for grad studies or law school. But in the library, where I should have been studying for my exams, I was poring through the work of Diane Arbus and Robert Frank. I was trying to hone my own vision of the authentically exotic out of nothing but a fear of ending up in the suburbs—a salary man, as they called the type in Japan, with a mortgage, and a marriage drained of any real passion.

I lived in fear of revealing any of it to my parents. They had both emigrated to Canada from Holland, my father after the war as a young veteran of Dunkirk and my mother more than a decade later. For them my father's steady work as a machinist at an auto parts manufacturer, complete with health benefits for the whole family, and the three-room bungalow they were able to buy in a small suburban town was worth all the hellish years they had lived through when they were young. My father was almost into his forties when he finally met my mother, and he never spoke about what he did during the war or his years of wandering in Canada, working on farms, doing cheap manual labour. He wanted to draw a curtain on the past and keep his young family in the bright rooms of the present tense. He believed I was going to photograph innocent campus "hijinks" (his word, mispronounced with his Dutch accent) with the camera he had gotten in the seventies for our family trip to Banff and had never really used since. If he had had any idea that I had been spending my last break week before graduation photographing underground parking lots and abandoned factories in Toronto, to capture images suggestive of post-industrial ruin, I was not sure whether he would have been disappointed or amused.

And now there was really no way to know. When I visited him, I realized so much of his more recent past was eroding. Remembered images were mixing with hallucinations that might have had some significance, some purchase in reality, long ago. As my bus from Toronto slowed along the highway, closing in on the exit, I looked out at the stretch of cornfields, the rows of stalks fading from bone white to a darker golden hue, the edges of the leaves tinged tobacco brown. My father's room in his care facility looked out on cornfields, too, but what did he see? A leafy stretch of the Merwede river, in the Dordrecht of his youth?

I had travelled to my father's hometown some years before, in search of some clues to what the world of his youth might have been like. On that trip I had spent time in the Jordaan neighbourhood in Amsterdam where my mother had grown up, as well. By then I had saved and bought a beautiful old Leica in a specialty shop in Shinjuku. I decided I would make it a personal project to photograph streetscapes and buildings that had survived the war. I told them about the trip, but I never did share the photos I took.

I suppose I was ashamed to reveal how the results really did not transcend tourist cliché. Here I was, more than a decade on, and I still couldn't say I had managed anything close to a breakthrough in my efforts to make something like art. The poetry of the moment, as they say, was as elusive for me as any powerful connection to the past.

And yet, every time I come out to this town, every time I see them, I bring these photos along, with my two cameras and my notebooks in my backpack. A long time ago I had resolved to go through all those photos with both my parents. That was before my father's diagnosis.

My mother now lives in a small condominium in the newer part of Milton. It's close to the bus station; it's close to everything downtown she might need. The developer and his advertised team of architects took the old administrative offices of the auto parts plant and turned them into something that looks like a cheap hotel for salesmen on the road. The glass, chrome and mahogany trim everywhere still give off a faint odour of glue, but the place is already starting to look old and shabby. An effort to erase one identity from the building's past has only made it more apparent. To enter the building with my mother, carrying half her groceries, is to see her gait and her very posture change from one of an independent woman in the world to a frail tenant on the periphery of someone's dubious effort at contemporary living. She's so nervous and self-conscious about the video cameras mounted on the ceiling.

I entered the front antechamber and poked one finger at the right combination of numbers and letters on the intercom system. As I waited for her muffled voice and the sound of the buzzer, I too felt diminished and trapped in a cell, waiting for the camera eye to swivel above me. I thought of Nataša, in a real cell somewhere perhaps, and moved to the door, focused on the elevator, metres away, my heart pounding with violent rage at her captor.

Every time I see my mother she looks smaller. She was always slender, and in the photographs taken of her as a young woman in Amsterdam, she looked like a young ballet dancer, so elegantly poised, her long blond hair swept up and tied back from her broad forehead. Now she makes me think of a frail little bird. As she gripped my arms before we embraced, her wristwatch looked like it could slip right off her hand. When I was in university and indeed even when I had come back for a visit after my first year in Tokyo, she always asked if I were eating properly and would even probe a little further, inquiring about my last dinner. Now it was my turn to ask as soon as we embraced.

She led me into her sitting room where I took my place on the old couch, with its dowdy floral pattern. The royal blue settee from the house where I grew up. These pieces were mixed in with two new end tables she had surely picked up from a discount outlet near the highway. She had fortunately made a little bit of money with the sale of the house. Neither Henrik nor I worry about her burning through what's in the bank though. Since my father has gone into the care facility, she has been living like she is in wartime again, eating chocolate sandwiches and canned soup.

"I don't understand why you're the only person looking for this student of yours, Lucien. She had no friends?"

"She has friends of course. But they are elsewhere."

She did not try to conceal the look of concern on her face. She began to speak, hesitated, then carried on, even though there was a quaver in her voice. "I don't know why you don't let the police do their job."

"I would be happy to. I don't think they have a sense of how urgent this is."

"People disappear all the time."

"That's right, I guess. But I'm not prepared to accept she will."

It was inevitable, her next question. She was looking down at her stockinged feet in her white Scholls, biting her lip in the same way I catch myself doing. *Henrik's his father's boy and you, you have so much of me, Lucien.*

"Do you care for this girl, Lucien?"

"Woman, Mama. This woman's name is Nataša." Yes, it was freighted with all of the unspoken disappointment she, and possibly my father, felt about the dissolution of my relationship with Keiko. I know she had been hoping for a grandchild. They had gotten to know Keiko and were almost comfortable with the idea that she and I might make a life for ourselves in Japan when I broke things off and mystified everyone. Well, here was a try at a little less mystification. "I think I do care for her, yes, Mama. She was no longer coming to class when we first went on a date. We were very careful. But then she broke it off."

"I see. Then you must be very upset." She crossed her legs and tilted her gaze up at me, examining me in profile. Maybe she was looking for an indication of deception.

"I don't know how much time I have to find her. That's why I came out to you in such a rush."

"I see. I understand."

She rose from the couch and walked into her kitchen, where I could see the keys to the Regal on one of the hooks of her key holder. A souvenir of the Black Forest, of all places. Henrik bought it for them after one of his first trips abroad with his varsity soccer team. I always wondered how they could take in the lacquered photo of the German countryside—the wartime *Heimat*—along with the Gothic font and not want to hide such a thing away forever.

"Lucien, could you do one thing for me? Could you visit your father before you leave?"

"Mama, you know I'd love to go see him. But it's three o'clock.

I mean by the time I get there, they will probably be having dinner."

"I just think . . . You know it's his car. He loved that car. And if I told him you took it without telling him first, he might be upset. I'd feel terrible."

I wanted to cut her off. A younger me, one I'd like to think was capable of being more difficult than I am now, probably would have and said what I was thinking—that we couldn't even be sure if Dad remembered he had that car, never mind whether he could have cared that I took it. But no, I didn't. I nodded, said that I understood.

"Besides, it's close to dinner. You should eat and stay the night. Best to see him in the morning and set off."

I nodded, looking out her window at the traffic. There were two cars idling at the stoplight, and there was the faint sound of heavy metal rock radio coming from one of them. Some things would never change about this town. Every time I was here I fought an urgency within me to bolt, get out as soon as I could and get back into the city, the present tense.

"I have a couple of minute steaks. We can have dinner here, *ja*?" She was smiling wanly. And I, looking like her more every day, I suppose, smiled wanly and nodded again.

11. Nataša Ružić: Notebook One

"Please do not put anything down toilet but TOILET PAPER," says the sign on the door. I have been warned, I suppose. The man behind the counter of the motel told me to call him Roy, and I'm quite sure this is his writing. He has a homemade tattoo on his forearm, a torpedo with "Diane" and "RCAF" written along the length of it, and the lettering is similar to what's on the sign. As he walked me down to my room he said he has had heart surgery, so I better not cause him any trouble. He called me a gypsy and that's exactly what I hoped for. I told them my name was Magda László, because I figured Roy and Vesna, his wife, who works the counter, might not recognize the name of an opera singer when they heard it. They didn't, but Roy, with a weird crooked grin on his face, asked me if I had seen the movie *Casablanca*. Then Vesna took my cash without asking for any ID, as Gina my new doughnut-shop friend had told me she would. Vesna's fingernails are painted blood red. She flicked through the bills carefully and then nodded to Roy. As Roy walked me to the room he demanded I show him my arms, my calves and ankles. "No junkies, no meth-heads, and no crack whores. You cook up and start a fire, I'll let you burn. Vesna and me will come out ahead if this whole place goes up in flames." Then he slid the key across the counter—he wanted minimal physical contact. "TV don't work. Sorry about that."

Couples like Roy and Vesna always fascinate me. What brought them together? What keeps them together? It seems different from love but more enduring. Call it a shared survival strategy. At one crucial point in their lives they must have realized they could do better together, faced with their options, than they could apart. And they have remained in their battle positions long after the end of their war with the world.

I called Dejan from a gas station payphone this morning, promptly at 10 a.m., as I promised. He tells me his call with Petar and Nikola went exactly as we thought it would. Nikola fell into his old lieutenant's role and tried to be stern with Dejan, angry about the night of the blackout. Petar was silent. It was only when Dejan defended himself, saying at least he had the guts to get on a plane and try to handle the situation with the video clip, that Petar expressed something like support: "That is true." Such a brave one, Petar—he is still scared that Caroline will find out about any of this. And he still won't commit to selling off some of the fakes Alex made for Caroline so that he can get us our money. Dejan might not be right about much, but he's right about Petar. He's whipped. They could not agree on anything except for what we already know: there is no way Lazarević can find the money, but he affirmed he would be the only one to respond to me. However, both he and Petar are skeptical that will be necessary. They believe either I'll go to the police or the police will find me before Dejan can try to handle things correctly, as he said, once again.

When he said "correctly" on the phone, I don't think Dejan was conscious of being ironic. I don't think he's capable of that.

Still, for now, I am necessary for his survival strategy, and he is mine. It almost makes me sad when he tries to find the words to make it into something more. He says that he can't wait until we're together again. How touching. You be my Roy and I'll be your Vesna.

I have got maybe an hour to put one word after another, to write this, and another email for Uncle Milan. I'm looking out onto a courtyard of broken patio stones, a chain-link gate that frames a view of the lake, two layers of washed-out green under the sky for a horizon today—the lawn and the waves. I'm trying to figure out the words. There's so much to explain to dear Uncle Milan. I have to write my note in such a way that he keeps it to himself, doesn't go to the police, doesn't even share it with that horrible wife of his, who has always hated me. "Uncle Milan, I'm asking you to be my saviour." *And keep our conversation secret until I come to you.* A simple message, plainly delivered, but there is so much to tell and where to start. All I really want to do is sleep for a week.

Of course he'll read the newspapers and see my name. And once he gets my message, he'll start going into Alex's career, the paintings, the controversies. *Why would you ever agree to pose for a man like that?* Uncle Milan, I have always been asking for trouble, haven't I? It is not as if anyone expected more from me.

Those words could be an epitaph, I know, so before I transform from the Nataša I was, I want to keep one promise I made to her: try to be honest, at least to myself. Call it *The Brief History of Nataša Ružić.* This is the highlights reel.

I was born. It was in Sarajevo in 1973, and that's where I grew up too. I arrived the day before Christmas. My father, Ivo, who was, as he described himself, vaguely Orthodox, and whose family is from Zagreb, liked to say it was a good omen. He was full of such thoughts and superstitions. Once I was out into the world my mother, Damira, who was from a little Bosnian village called Foča, was thankful she could sleep through a Christian holiday and recover from the worst pain she had ever felt. She told me when I was a teenager, warning me away from childbirth and revising her own past to suggest she had always truly been Muslim and had a distaste for Christian holidays.

I have my father's eyes. I know I also have his love of harsh cigarettes, his dark hair, and his long legs. I have my mother's laugh, her love of sugar, the same creases on my face from smiling and squinting in the sun (though I don't think I've done much of either here), the same streak of independence—as my father called it, wilfulness. I am an only child. I suppose I'm an only adult, now that they are both gone.

Given the circumstances, I like to think of Natašas one and two as failed experiments. Not a bad set of genes to start with: two intelligent parents—at one time my mother was considered a prominent academic and political activist—but both were victims of bad timing, if you like. As I suppose Lucien and I were as well.

"Make your opportunities," Uncle Milan once said to me. I will.

I can feel Vesna circling, starting to get suspicious about how much time this new gypsy whore is taking, scaring away everybody else from the breakfast room. First Vesna walked by with a mop and bucket, smiling, then she passed with a skeleton key, and now she is watching me carefully through a window where she thinks I can't see her. I have been procrastinating long enough. I dread writing this letter to Uncle Milan too. But I must get that one done.

It is all very clear, at least in my head. He's going to know about my disappearance if he reads the newspapers, it is not as if I have to go into much detail about that. I'm fine, unhurt, I'll reassure him that I haven't been abducted. And he'll understand when I say I can't go to the police, we have our own shared history of how useless they can be protecting anyone from those who are determined to hunt you down. All I want him to know is that I'm coming to him. Simple, forthright, as direct as I could ever be.

Still I think about what I could say to Milan about Petar, Nikola, and even Dejan. I could show him the clip. Maybe that would be the right thing to do. I feel I owe my loyalty to Dejan. I may come to owe him so much more. I only fear he might ask me for love, and I am clearly capable of many things, but not that. Not now.

Before Vesna approaches me—no more thinking, get the words on the screen. A little truth and a little fiction, all within an hour. I may not be getting better at honesty, but I'm at least more efficient.

12. Christina Perretti

I came to Canada from Milan primarily because of Georg Barany and Caroline Vidler. It is a curious thing about my line of work: it becomes like you're working in a small village. Those who are involved in the theft and forgery of art all connect through the same dealers and intermediaries to either legitimize or authenticate the goods for sale. I knew Barany and Vidler were quite a team. I couldn't pin anything on them yet.

I also knew they had a long-standing relationship with Alex Rebane. Curiously for a dealer and gallerist of her profile, Vidler had never put a show together for Rebane in her own space.

Equally curious was her relationship with her boyfriend and new business partner Petar Stepanović. Though he had cultivated a following for his art and enjoyed a brief period of local fame in Montreal, Vidler had never shown his work either.

Stepanović had been quite open about his time in Serbia before coming to Canada as a refugee. Indeed he had based more than one of his pieces on his experience as a soldier. As I began to investigate through my colleagues with Interpol, I discovered they had an open file on him, as part of a larger network of suspected war criminals and gangsters—many from the former Eastern Bloc. The US government was investigating this group for a list of crimes, from human trafficking to the hacking of a series of porn sites for credit card information and, presumably, identity theft and fraud.

All of it was of interest to me. The more I spoke to the Canadian police, the more I found them resistant to following up on any of it. They had no one working in art crimes, and Detective Fortune, though he would tell me he was communicating with the RCMP and CSIS, would tell me nothing of value. I was beginning to think they really didn't want to look into Rebane's death much further.

It was either a question of resources or a question of politics, given their greater interest in the parking attendant. I decided it was not for me to determine. I had enough to go on to interview Barany, that's all that mattered. I was happy to get out of that city and to travel to Montreal, happy to leave them to their own dubious conclusions.

13. Alex Rebane

Dear M.,

One week until my show opens at Renzo Casale's new place on Ossington, and I can hear the gears of the old sausage-making machine begin to crank and groan. I am going to be served up once more for our esteemed dinner guests before what's left of me gets thrown to the dogs. I envy you the company that dined on your work: Cardinal del Monte, papal jurists, men of the Curia, princes and courtiers, and of course, a couple of popes themselves, with their special relationship with Nobodaddy. I can barely get a Governor General in this bloody country to commission a portrait. But we can't choose the age in which we're born, just like we can't choose our family. I've done what I could with what I've got. You had your prostitute Madonna, and I've got my refugee waif coming to stay with me and be my little muse. And now, with Imperial Travesties opening, I know I'm headed for a summing up.

I know Caroline and Barany can sense it coming too. They want to squeeze every last penny from the wet paint on my brushes. Barany's contacted me about one last job (it's always one last job): three works for his new client Mikha in upstate New York. Barany will arrange the details, he says. All I have to do is get the fakes and store them in the old boathouse when I'm done. Caroline is of course in on it as well, but she's even more excited about how much press the headscarf Nataša paintings are getting. She said a filmmaker gentleman named Theo van Gogh (yes, an actual relation) is interested in putting all of them in a film he's making. That could triple their market value, she says. They both know it means I'll soon be rich enough to say no to everything once again, and they're right. Once I have my fuck-off money, I'm done.

It was fun for a while though. I understand the attraction the demimonde had for you. I liked the dinners with the Russians and the Serbian thugs, Caroline's Eurotrash clientele. There's life to them; they're risking everything every day. There was no way I was ever going to come back as legitimate for the new guard—same as the old guard in their love of all things new and empty. Too much of the sick soul of Europe in me. I love what Nataša has done for my work too. She's like a little puzzle that's impossible to solve. I've even sensed that, with Barany, lurking behind his charlatan act there is a very sharp mind and something of an artist in him too. I know that at the bottom of it all there is nothing but bad money and poisonous politics.

Here's the worst of it, I want out because I wouldn't mind discovering if I can live with myself again: clean, doing no harm to anyone, maybe even being good to people. People like Nataša.

I can hear you laughing. How can I be so naive after all I've been through. I've known the terms from the very beginning, even when I could imagine my rise and fall had something to do with my talent and when the rich weren't quite so criminal. I've said yes to everything that has brought me here, especially the forgeries Barany and Caroline have paid me so well for over the years. And I took pleasure in my contempt for their clients, and found in them something like friendship. Honour among thieves and all that. I sat and drank with those ugly Russian friends of Barany's, knowing full well that it was probably their fathers and grandfathers who made orphan refugees of my parents. And yes, it felt a little like payback to take their ill-gotten money. I suppose no one knows better than you that you can't want as much as I've wanted—the claim to legitimacy, to be authentic in an inauthentic world—without paying for it.

Truly, when I think of where I want to be in a decade I know it's far from this dirty little city, far from everyone. A beach, some pretty boys in a bar every now and then, and painting for no one but myself. I know that's what you would have wanted too, and I swear, if it all goes as planned, I'm going to get there sooner than I thought. I dare you to tell me you would play all of it any differently.

I'll write you again soon, old friend.

A.

14. Lucien Bollinger

I dread these visits to my father in his new home, despite the fact that I like to think that I returned from Tokyo after all these years because of his situation. Even when I begin to speak about it I drift into euphemisms, comfortable language to deal with the disease that's killing him. It's a situation that offers no comfort or consolation at all. But my presence does matter, if only because the thought of him alone in his facility (read bedlam), with only my mother to visit him, is unbearable. They are separated, and that is tragic enough, but they are also exiled, cast out into this strange netherworld where neither can live in the home they once had together.

The time I spend with him marks a crossing through the borderland of memory, of rational, predictable, ordinary life, into the rapidly eroding landscape of his inner world, where fragments of dreams and hallucinations are like channels on a TV that his mind flips through in random succession. And he's not watching from his chair or his bed in his spare quarters; he's crossed through to the other side of the screen like he's passed through a mirror. Sometimes his world seems a reflection of the reality he's living, and then he vanishes somewhere else. The unnerving part is that he still recognizes me, assimilates me into his waking dream. I am like a formerly recurring character who makes a cameo appearance among a cast of unknowns. And then, like the shifting screens of a kabuki play, he is back in the present tense as we both experience it.

Yet it is even worse for my mother to visit him because, within his fragmented realities, she often recognizes names and images he mentions from their shared memories—people they once knew, places they have been together. Once when she arrived in his room he was angry with her because he had lost his watch, and he accused her of having taken it from him the day before, as they were in the apartment building across the road from the facility. None of that happened, of course, but what made it worse was that he described where it occurred, and the building's lobby became the lobby of the old Molou cinema in Haliburton, where they watched movies one summer as newlyweds. In moments like these she is reminded of the man she fell in love with and aches to pull him back into her world.

Strangeness and belonging. I had lived more than a decade abroad in a city where I would never feel at home, and I thought that validated my transformed sensibility. In Tokyo I had been training my eye to recognize the authentic and to reject cliché, in a city of pastiche that subsumed and digested and refashioned everything I recognized as kitsch at home. Now here I was in the town where I was born, right back where I started from, writing my name at the visitor's desk and seeing the similarities between my handwriting and my father's. I was so close to familiar things, in a place devoted to maintaining some semblance of normal for the true travellers into the unknown and the defamiliarized. How callow my ambition seemed in comparison to the journey of all these residents.

My father is on the floor of the advanced cases. I could walk out of the elevator with my eyes shut and know I'm on the right level simply because of the voices, how loud they are. There is a shrieking woman relegated to a wheelchair at the end of the corridor who is only louder because of her distance from the rest of them. Another woman in her sixties patrols the halls, wearing a Tom Jones t-shirt (where does anyone find that for their mother?), carrying a half-naked doll and waving frantically every time she sees me because I spoke with her once. She says the doll is her baby and that she's getting married to Tom Jones next week, always next week. There is the larger man in mismatched sweats who shuffles from table to table in the breakfast area, his bristly white hair shooting out from the crown of his head as if he's electrified. He has the thick, gnarled fingers of a man who once worked hard with his hands for a living, a crude tattoo on his forearm that is simply a name—Dražen. It looks like it was etched with cheap ink in a prison. The institutional setting, with pale green walls and the smell of cheap laundry soap, might even be familiar to him, perhaps a consolation. He has shuffled over with an air of menace on the few occasions my father and I have sat in the breakfast area, and he grins and chortles to himself. I always try to block out my fears for my father's safety when I see him glaring back, his unblinking watery eyes offering the sternest challenge he can muster. The courage it must take to live among all this madness . . . No wonder he retreats to the world of dreams and flickering memories.

And yet I can't deny my own interest and attentiveness to what is revealed, now that my father is in this state. He never spoke about his wartime experiences when I was growing up, the door closed on that part of his past. My mother had told me he was briefly imprisoned in Holland, escaped, ended up in Dunkirk, was evacuated and then re-enlisted in the British forces, ending up as a tail-gunner who had managed to survive D-Day. His menacing floormate Dražen probably pales in comparison to what my father might once have feared. But if he has relived any old trauma, no one on staff here has mentioned it to my mother or me. The war years are revealed in the old songs he trills to himself in his thick Dutch accent. *Bloo-bedz over ze vhite clifz of Dov-uh.* Last time I was here he looked out a window in the breakfast room and saw those cliffs in the quarry on the escarpment, a few miles in the distance.

As I approached his door my thoughts went again to Nataša. By the time we had sat down for our second date, as it were—a cup of bad coffee in the Chinese restaurant a block from the school where I taught her night class—she, through nervous laughter, told me she had ended up in London after the war. My first thought was that she had stumbled over her words, she couldn't have meant that war, the experience that cast its long shadow of silence over the brightly coloured rooms of my family home growing up. But of course not, she hadn't stumbled at all. There was only one war in the whole of history for her. As it had for both my parents, the war, her war had erased her family and scrawled a dark black line, like a thick brush stroke down the middle of a painting, between the world of her childhood and the wider world left for her to wander through like an unquiet ghost.

It attracted me. How much of my infatuation with her was tied to the riddle of an absence, and was this inextricably connected to the mystery of the lost years of my father's life, those I feared would never be recovered now? Whether I liked it or not, had my father's trauma shaped my own identity, sent me looking for a lover who would complete me, her trauma near the surface rather than submerged for a generation?

There was no response when I knocked on my father's door, so I walked in. Everything was as I expected: he was sitting in one of the visitors' chairs at the window, staring out into the distance. An attentive nurse had put a tartan blanket on his lap, and it draped down to cover his bare legs. He probably needed a little warmth, he was only wearing a ratty old bathrobe and his underwear, and the temperature on his floor always seems to hover somewhere around twenty degrees. I called his name and finally he turned to me, with his mouth hanging open, a soft downy covering of grey bristles on his haggard face.

"Lucien, I was just calling you."

"Well there you are, Papa. I'm here."

I bent over and awkwardly embraced him. His frame and brittle bones had shrunk so much it was like holding onto a boy. *The father becomes the son.*

"Where did you go?"

"Go? Um. I guess I was in Toronto."

This seemed to upset him. He knitted his brow and looked away from me, as if there were a scene of greater interest out there somewhere past the suburban sprawl. "I don't know what you look for there."

Look for. As if I was a boy who had gone wandering and ended up far from home. Maybe he wasn't so wrong about that, really.

"Neither do I, I guess. There was a blackout there. All the lights. Did you get it here?"

He nodded and gave me a stern look as if I was asking him a silly question, talking nonsense, as he used to say.

"Of course they must go out." He raised his hand as if to poke a hole in the air above his head. "The Stukas . . . You want to give them a target in the night?"

I shook my head and smiled. "No, you're right, Papa."

"You're like your mother. Head in the clouds." He shook his head and looked down at his cheap beige slippers. They were the same ones he had when I was in university, so many years ago. A Father's Day gift I had bought with my student-loan money. "And where is she?"

My first impulse was to say she was at home. But of course that wasn't really true. It would be as valid as saying he was now too.

Every time I had visited him before he had had enough presence of mind to tell me he hated where he was, that he was ready to go home. I could only nod in acknowledgement, fearing his simmering look of incrimination, like I was complicit in his current state of detention. I suppose I was.

"She's resting today. But she gave me the car to come up and see you. The Regal."

His gaze went back to the window. He nodded, refusing to look at me.

"She suggested I check with you about one thing. I'm going to need it for a few days."

"Need what?"

"The car."

"Jonny Betenhuis drove by out there this morning. He was in a 2CV. He's selling suits from the trunk. And shirts from Jermyn Street."

"From Jermyn Street?"

"French cuffs. Too big for me. He wants to sell them to the Yankees. Jonny's never going to change."

I nodded and smiled. I was suddenly hopeful, anticipating the moment of connection I had been hoping for. I reached into my backpack and pulled out a stack of black and white photos tucked into a small white envelope.

"I think he might be in one of these shots. I took them with your old Compax, Papa. Remember that camera?"

He glared at me once again. "Why, did you lose it?"

"No, no. I still have it. It still works."

"Of course it works. That camera cost me two hundred dollars. We don't buy rubbish in this house, you understand?"

"I understand."

"I had four shirts from Jermyn Street and a smoking from Savile Row. I married your mother in that suit."

I smiled for him. "From Jonny Betenhuis?"

"Not from Jonny Betenhuis. You don't be smart!"

I laughed, pulled a few photos out from the white envelope and one by one, handed them to him. "You see? Here's Dordrecht. Here's your street. There's the house where you were born."

His brow was furrowed, and it seemed as though the broken blood vessels on his cheeks flushed a darker shade of purple. He'd been a heavy smoker for fifty years. He examined the photos one by one, transfixed and frowning. I was watching him closely, in case tears started to well up in his glassy, grey-blue eyes. I've inherited those eyes, maybe even his gaze. After I handed him the last one he exhaled, placed the stack in his lap, and then once again looked out the window, silent.

"You should take these away."

"Pardon, Papa?"

"Take these away! And you should go."

My heart began to race. I had displeased him, I was in trouble. I was four years old again. "Papa, what do you mean?"

"You think you trick your father? It's Marian, that nurse with the fat ass. She got you to come in here."

"No, Papa!'

"You should be ashamed of yourself. You think I don't know Dordrecht? I was born there. You show me fake photos so I tell you my secrets. You betray your father."

"I swear, Papa."

He raised his arm and pointed to the door. He was wide-eyed, enraged. "Get out! Get out! You traitor!" He flung the photos at me and they scattered on the floor.

I want to say I calmly picked them all up, called for his nurse, and quietly left the room. I want to say I was calm, not shaking, not crying like a child again. I hurried out of his room and bolted for the elevator, not looking back.

I guess he never really gave me permission to take his car either. But I lied to my mother and said he did. *Traitor.*

15. Milan Zujović

No matter what you say about who was right and who was wrong, there is a central fact: for all of us who survived what happened in the nineties in Serbia, Croatia, and Bosnia, life has become a three-volume book. The first volume is the life before, the second is the war, the third is the life after, and even for the most fortunate and untouched by tragedy there is very little each volume has in common with the others. Every now and then, there will be moments of recognition, when the life before suddenly collides with the life after, and it can lead you to rewrite your three volumes in your head.

What I suppose I mean here is that sometimes, just like Cassandra in the play, sometimes you see ghosts. It is never quite clear to me whether they are from the past or the future, like the spirits that poor girl saw, but these visitations do their work on you, no question.

My most recent encounter was with a ghost right here in Vancouver. My wife Mira and I had finished rehearsals at around ten one night. It was during our second week here. On our way to a restaurant we had to pick up Rebecca, our lighting designer, who was joining us. She was staying with her father in a condominium in the neighbourhood they call Yaletown. As the taxi pulled up to the building Rebecca wasn't answering her cell phone, so I told

Mira I would go up to the front desk and ask if they could buzz her for me.

The security person working as a kind of concierge was an older man. He looked a little awkward in his ill-fitting uniform, manning the phone. But as I approached he looked up and recognized me. It was as though those icy blue eyes lit up. He started to smile, and then, as if in shame, thought better of it. I knew from his face—I can't really explain it—that he was from back home.

I asked him to ring for Rebecca, and he complied with a soldier's nod. The backs of his big hands were wrinkled and had blotchy, pale brown freckles that betrayed his age. As we waited in silence for Rebecca to come down, he decided to risk what he wanted to say.

He addressed me with a brusque "hey, *poeta*," a word that doesn't quite translate as poet. It has a wider meaning, more of an honorific, as you say, than the other word we have, *pesnik*.

He introduced himself as Nikola, and I asked him if we might have met each other back home. He said he didn't think so, but he knew of my work, and why I was in town.

"Your play, is it any good?"

I said I wasn't sure or some such thing, while I tried to place him. The more I stood there waiting for Rebecca in the awkward silence, the more I felt I should recognize who he was.

"Maybe I will go and see it, judge for myself, yes?"

I told him that would probably be a good idea, and then the elevator doors opened and there was Rebecca at last. I shook his hand as we left, and we wished each other well in our language.

Still, something about him and the silence between us haunted me for days after. It still does. He was a ghost, someone from that book we all like to keep closed.

As part of my work on *The Blood of Agamemnon*, I was looking at old films that take on classical tragedies. My favourite remains

Cocteau's *Orphée*. There is a scene where Orpheus walks through a mirror into the land of the dead. This is what encounters with people like this Nikola feel like—someone gazing at you from the other side of the mirror, behind your reflection. It is probably why I put so many mirrors in the House of Agamemnon on stage. They are where Cassandra can see the ghosts.

I wonder if Nikola did get to the play. I wish we could have spoken of the work and what he thought. *Hey* poeta: he said those words in a way that only men of our generation address each other, familiar, almost affectionate but too full of irony for such an open-hearted feeling.

As I get older, I think of who the ideal audience is—something the marketing people and their sycophants, including artistic directors in some theatres, will ask. More and more I realize my ideal audience consists of ghosts like that old man, sitting there in his awkward uniform of new citizenship in some building thousands of miles away from the life he once knew, with too much time to think about the past and too little to gain to walk through the mirror and join the living again.

16. Lucien Bollinger

I did not want to go to Alex's funeral. I barely knew him, and if the opening of his show had been any indication of the company he kept, I was happy to remain a stranger to his world. But the time I spent with the police made me feel less than confident in their abilities to track Nataša down. If anyone could give me a lead on where she could have gone it was Caroline Vidler and Petar Stepanović; they were the only strong contacts in Canada that Nataša had.

They were there, of course, walking down the aisle of an old Lutheran church as if they had both walked away from a car crash. And maybe they were truly grieving, who knows? Caroline's tears during the funeral were convincing. Great actors, both of them. Perhaps they always had to be, given their vocations, and in that sense they were the perfect match.

I had an uneasy feeling throughout the service. I was in one of the first pews, compelled to keep my eyes on the casket and on the minister at his lectern. I felt someone's gaze on me throughout, but every time I cast a furtive glance over at Caroline and Petar they too were focused on the proceedings.

Afterwards, as I approached Caroline on the steps of the church, we embraced and she gently tapped my wrist.

"Lucien, Renzo Casale and I have put together a small reception at the Estonian Hall for those who have travelled for this. I know it's what Alex would have wanted. You must come."

Once there, I could only justify my presence at the reception by paying my condolences to Alex's parents. They orbited the wake far from each other, as if magnetically repelled. His mother, a shrunken figure with dyed orange hair, was dressed in black silk like the widow of a mob boss. When she discovered who I was from my awkward introduction, she ignored me, busying herself with a proffered tray of smoked salmon on little discs of pastry. It was the same with Alex's father, a grey-faced accountant who moved like sadness had wintered in him for years. The old man looked me in the eye briefly before he nodded, gazing at the shiny toecaps of his polished shoes, and walked out of the cavernous hall without a word.

I fared no better with the crowd Alex referred to as the Forest Hill Chamber of Commerce—too rich and respected to be considered louche. They huddled in fours and sixes, the smell of expensive perfumes like markings in the snow outside little tents of gossip, a tactic employed to keep mongrels like me away.

Only the never-quite-made-it friends of Rebane's, those who knew the catering staff by name, were approachable and, a minute into a rambling, pointless conversation with some burnout, I realized I was in for a long night if I stayed among this crowd until the taxis began to arrive.

It was a relief to find Caroline and Petar once again, out on the front steps, smoking furiously. They were only too willing to talk about Nataša.

"She was never a gallery assistant. She was an admin assistant." Caroline cupped her wine glass and brought it to her lips. But before she could sip, another point had to be made. "She would have needed some rudimentary understanding of painting to be a gallery assistant."

"And she didn't."

"No, she certainly did not." She cast a quick glance over at Petar leaning on the stone staircase. His lips were pursed, his arms folded high against his chest. "I'm stating a fact, Petar."

Petar tilted his head and gave a quick nod. Like her he had decided to take his drinks outside with him. He had placed his shot of Aquavit and a bottle of beer on the wide railing of the staircase. He cast suspicious glances at both, as if unsure whether there might be poison in one or the other.

"If we had known she would skip off to model with Alex, we would have thought twice about sponsoring her for her work visa. Am I right?"

Petar nodded once more, and then his phone went off. He reached into his jacket and yanked it out, cupping it over his mouth. It didn't sound like he was speaking English as he moved away from us, beer in hand, nodding solemnly to Caroline.

"Now please take this the right way. I mean I'm sorry for what's happened, and we both hope and pray she's found alive soon. But I have my suspicions she's more than all right. There is the small matter of Alex's missing money."

"There was money stolen?"

"The cops didn't tell you? We told them. We saw his suitcase in their photos when they interviewed us."

"They didn't talk about that with me, no."

Caroline lit another cigarette from the end of the one she had been smoking. Her hands were quivering, but she stilled herself with a deep drag and looked up at the overcast sky. She was deciding how much she was going to tell me, I realize now. Maybe she actually believed what she was about to say.

"Alex told me years ago that when he first made money from his paintings, he took the battered old suitcase he brought with him down to New York and filled it with sixty thousand dollars in cash. That was what he made from his first show down there. He always told himself he was going to save that until he really needed it. But then came the drugs, and he dipped into it over a few months and it was gone. Anyway, this time around, as a promise to himself that he'd stay clean, he filled that suitcase up with American bills once more."

"If the amount was based on the sale of his paintings now, it must have been more than sixty thousand dollars."

"That might be. The point is that the money is gone. And I guarantee you that's why we haven't heard from Nataša. She can buy herself some time before she turns up on her own terms."

"You make it sound like you think she might have . . ." I couldn't even get the words out of my mouth. That was not the Nataša I had fallen in love with.

"I'm no cop, darling. I know what I know. Last time I spoke with them, they seemed to believe there's some radical Muslim out there who is Alex's murderer. The bottom line is that they've got a theory, and a concern, that she's not going to be found."

"Alive. You can say it. I've said it in my head often enough. They don't believe she's going to be found alive."

"Have they recommended that you take any kind of counselling right now? God, I know I'd be with my therapist every day."

"Not the guys I dealt with, no. I guess that's for afterwards. At first they treated me like a suspect, to be honest."

"Fucking cops. They're the same in Montreal. One rung up from the criminals."

"My problem is she spoke so little of her life in London and in Sarajevo. When I asked her she would say what's past is past, and change the subject."

"Did she ever speak of us to you?"

"She said she owed you both so much. You got her over here, gave her a chance at a new life."

"One thing you should know . . . She wasn't quite stable, you know? She was in trouble in London."

"She never told me."

"No, I imagine not. She could be a little creative with the truth. You know she was an actress?"

"When she was younger. She told me she wanted to write. We had a few conversations about that. She wanted to tell the story of what she went through."

"I'll offer you my perspective, Lucien. I of course have not known Nataša for any length of time compared to Petar. I was simply trying to help someone. When Petar returned from London last year—it was March, he had gone over to do some research. He knew where he could get old videos of the conflict in his country. He is still going to use them for a piece he is working on."

"She told me nothing about this."

"Ah. Well that's when I first heard of her. Petar told me she was an old friend. She was living in London and having a bit of a rough time. He said she might be coming over to give Canada a try. I needed someone in the gallery. My intern had buggered off to Morocco with her boyfriend, so it was timing, that was all it was."

"Still, that was good of you."

"No. I don't take charity cases. I try not to have noble intentions if I can avoid it. But I did all the paperwork with her visa. Once she arrived, after a few days in the gallery, she had done the impossible: she actually made me miss Julie, the intern who left."

"What do you mean?"

"The basics. Like showing up on time. Like being able to tell me who called and what they wanted. I wasn't asking for much. It wasn't soon after, anyway, that Alex came to town and we took him out. Nataša told me they hit it off. She said she thought they

had been lovers in a past life. She the man and he the woman."
Caroline tilted her head up and laughed. It seemed a gesture of a
woman so much older, something she had seen in an old movie.
"Isn't that something?"

"You think she was imagining more of a connection than
there actually was?"

"Let me tell you something, Lucien. Alex and I were actually
close. We had been for years. Nataša fascinated him, absolutely,
I'll give you that. Because she was a train wreck. She got very
theatrical with Alex, and he loved that. It was like a drag performance to him."

"She was never that way with me."

"No? Maybe she wanted different things from you, Mr. Bollinger."

"Maybe so."

"I'm very sorry for what you're going through. I mean, my
God, I hope they find her alive. But if you told me that she's going through something like a dissociative episode, that she's on the
streets somewhere, hearing voices in her head . . . It would not
surprise me. Even though I'm sure she had the presence of mind
to take that money."

"It's just that she seemed so indifferent to money. She even
spoke critically of Alex's attachment to it."

"Uh-huh. It's my experience that everyone's indifferent until
they really understand money. Until they really need it. This was
how I remember her too. I mean more than once the gallery doors
had been left open all night, the alarm not on. Can you imagine?
Millions of dollars in priceless work." Caroline shook her head,
ran her hand through the long strands of her hair. Still exasperated, it seemed. "The thing about Alex, what he didn't like to show,
was that broken people became projects for him. Understand, I'm
not saying his attraction to Nataša as a model wasn't sincere. But

people like Nataša came and went in his life. More than you could imagine. I'm sure she was convinced they had something special. He could make you feel that way, that you were the most interesting person in the world."

"Could he make you feel that way?"

"Ha!" Caroline took her last sip of wine. "But I am the most interesting person in the world. Ah, there's Petar. You'll excuse me."

I watched her head back into the front of the hall where Petar had emerged once again. With his swagger he really did seem like someone Caroline would soon tire of, as if he were her personal trainer rather than the video installation artist his website claimed he was.

She turned and looked back at me. "I really, really hope you find her."

"Thank you, Caroline. Thank you for your concern."

What else could I say? At that point I would take a little empathy anywhere I found it, regardless of how sincere it was.

There was very little to do at the Estonian Hall after that but feel sorry for myself and drink too many vodka and tonics.

As I stumbled out into the street I had that feeling of someone watching me once again. I pulled away in the old Regal and glimpsed the headlights of a car behind me flick on. It was a small, white economy model, a Nissan Sentra, one of the cheapest rentals you could get. I knew no one who would drive such a car.

I never should have gone to the funeral and then to the Estonian Hall. I should have taken Nataša's disappearance as a sign that there were greater forces at play than I could control. Vanity. I was less in love with the Nataša I knew than I was with my own nobility, my wilful disbelief that she might be someone else entirely.

17. Alex Rebane

Dear M.,

It is very late on an August night, and I can't sleep because of the heat, and I can't stand air conditioning. And I can't stand my paintings right now and I can't stand my life.

All this activity and none of it feels good for the soul. After a few hours on my new series with Nataša I have been working furiously to finish the two last Klees for Mikha, one of the new Russian friends. And in the meantime this vulgarian Petar is here, sharing my annex space to work on his ridiculous video installations. The sooner I get the Klees done, the sooner he will get out of here, and I can get back to a routine that doesn't feel like it's killing me.

To make the atmosphere in the house worse, there is something amiss with Nataša. She's sullen and even sarcastic with me. I questioned her about it, suggesting she might have had a tiff with her Lucien. The amanuensis. She snapped back a denial. "Lucien is incapable of making me this angry."

Her simmering rage has to be about Petar. Though he's wise enough to only spend a few hours a day here, I caught him and Nataša in a blazing argument, back in the annex. And whatever nonsense he's working on in there has made her curious. I've caught her snooping around in there while I make my first coffee in the morning. I let it go, though, and I even tried to make things up between us by being a little catty about Petar's work. I said I was risking more than I thought by trying to set him up for a show with Renzo. She gave me one of her weak little grins: "At least he's trying to make something authentic despite himself," she said.

I stopped myself from saying I wouldn't mind that as an epitaph. If she knows about my sideline I really don't care. She should get over herself and grow up. No one will be a saint for you, honey.

People. If you could only deal with them in silence. You could go on in solitude and have them hold still long enough for the work to get done. I'm sure you must have felt it too, that their dramas and their vanities are necessary because they're all recorded in the body, yet nothing good comes from any conversation that is not a simple transaction, and rarely enough even then.

Perhaps it's my mistake in becoming so close with Caroline. But I can't help but feel I would be dishonourable in deserting her. She was there when everyone else had walked away.

She is so fierce and unrepentant. I know you would have loved her too; an honest criminal is irresistible. When she first got me started working with Barany we got drunk on champagne together, and she told me she always had a feeling she would move into this sideline. She promises me that one day she'll tell me about her family and their scandalous past. I love a woman who respects tradition.

I'm sure she has some regrets about becoming so entwined in Petar's world though. What started as casual sex must have moved into a relationship only because of the greater transactional possibilities that Petar's network provided. Now she's dragged into an ongoing project of legitimizing him, and I'm too indebted to refuse her. This I would never say to her, but my God, it's never felt more tempting given the time he's here now. I've never earned my money more than I have now for him and his Russians.

As a reward for my struggles I'm going to get over to Rome once the Klees are done. I'm going to sit with your work for a few days and recharge. You're the only ally I have left. Perhaps I should be sadder about that.

I'll write you again soon.

A.

18. Nataša Ružić: Notebook One

A good night of sleep! I can't believe how long it has been. I came out of the hotel room and took in the sun, the cool, clean breeze, and now I truly feel, after the hellish drive, that I have been freed from Toronto.

Apparently I am near the border to the next province. After hours and hours on the road. I could have gone through four or five countries if I were in Europe—all this for the small fare of two hundred Canadian dollars. I handed the bills over ("twenties only, please") to my driver, Bruno, who told me this has become an almost regular thing for him when he drives to Winnipeg. He takes someone, working on a contract for our mutual friend Mikha. Bruno gets some company, a little walking-around money, as he called it, and his co-pilot doesn't have to worry about being tracked. "Everybody wins," he says. Everybody wins, that is, until you listen to what must be the complete Van Halen collection at least twice, until you try to wash yourself in three gas station washrooms, and until you have heard the full story of Bruno's life in Hamilton, Ontario. That includes every single thing Bruno remembers from the time he was twelve until now, with some discussion of his two divorces and his lost custody battle for his son, and the time he takes off the road caring for his mother, who is wheelchair-bound and has diabetes. Though he dropped me off in town, the one he recommended because it was "in the sticks but not too terrible," he told me we could link up again in Winnipeg, as he is driving farther west to Calgary. That is, if things don't work out on the next leg, when I ride with his good friend, a man named Gord Appleford, expected here tomorrow. I know I must be careful, that there is an effort to look for me, but I've made up my mind; I'm done with this. I'm going to walk into a bus station, buy a ticket and risk a trip through that province, then the next, then the next. I can picture Gord Appleford already and, well, no thanks. This country is like an American Siberia, and I would rather cross it alone.

I had a bad call with Dejan from a gas station payphone, and that didn't help matters. He said things did not go as well as he thought when he talked to Petar. Petar was at Alex's funeral, and couldn't talk, could not commit to getting the money from the last few fakes Alex had done for Barany and Caroline. Caroline has contacted Mikha in Buffalo, and he's ready to pick them up, and still Petar doesn't see what's happening as urgent. He said he hadn't even told Caroline about the request yet. What could I tell Dejan but that he had to try harder? It didn't go well. He asked me who Lucien was. The poor man had come to Alex's funeral and was pestering Caroline for all she could tell him about me. As soon as I tried to interject Dejan became impatient, interrogating me about how many times I had slept with Lucien, what he knew. I could barely reassure him that everything will be okay when we are together again. Be hopeful, we'll be starting a whole new life! It is like dealing with a child.

These pages are my only diversion. I can finally put some order and some thought to the time of my life I view as most important. Who did I become during the war years, and then with each decision I made once it was finally over? That time marked the dissolution of my parents' marriage, the formation of my ambitions, as naive and ridiculous as they seem to me now. It is strange, I realized, somewhere around the five-hundred-kilometre mark of my journey, that I view most of those years as the happiest in my life.

That is pathetic, when you think of what I've lived. If it is not reason enough for what they call a do-over here, on this side of the world, I really don't know what would be.

No matter where I begin in my thoughts, it all comes down to my Uncle Milan now.

I can only speak of how I came to know Milan, because I don't know what to trust from the accounts he gave me later, in our conversations—how he became the close friend of my parents. In all his stories he portrayed himself as a little wiser about the ways of the world than they were. Granted, that might not have been too difficult, considering the people my mother and father were, but it is only now, years later, that I have begun to question his version of their shared past.

He entered my life when I was in my first year of Nerkesija secondary school in Sarajevo. Nerkesija was in the old part of the city. I remember the ironwork on the staircases and the arched hallways, like something in an old Viennese hotel. I discovered, on my last visit there six years ago, that the high school is no longer there, though our old home is still standing, the stonework along the first floor of the apartment block pockmarked from bullet spray.

During that first year of high school, I had become withdrawn and quietly angry at the world. Life at home felt like a strange parlour game where we functioned with as little emotion as possible. We went on robotically, sharing the duties of preparing breakfast and dinner, cleaning the cramped apartment, emptying out the cat litter and keeping the little animal, Mejra, fed. We carried on the most banal conversations to pretend we were functioning like any other family. However, underneath my parents' attempt at civility with each other, I could sense their anger and sadness about what their marriage had become. They had drifted apart after our time in Michigan, where my father taught for two years, and where he became involved with another woman.

For years when I told people my English was good because of the time that we spent in America, no one believed me. Nothing but the language left its mark on me, it seems. But it's true: my father taught a first-year film course at Michigan State University, and the money was good enough that my mother and I could travel with him. She did post-graduate work there in the meantime. For her it was far better than teaching ninth-grade literature back home, bridling against the Soviet-style curriculum. "America will be a good change of pace, you'll see, Tašica" she said, though I suppose I was the only one in my family who did not feel eager to escape our lives.

I don't believe more than a few thousand people lived in East Lansing at the time, even though they called it a city. Like small towns everywhere, I suppose, everybody gets to know each other fast. My father was something of an attractive, exotic man to these young, impressionable women from small-town America, all his stories of shooting experimental films in the sixties, meeting Godard, Pasolini, and the one he called his mentor, Makavejev. It didn't take long in the fall semester before he started to cultivate a cool, detached air about him as he rediscovered his powers of seduction. But he was a terrible liar and a bumbling Don Juan; my mother caught on immediately.

I knew nothing about the customs around American Halloween then, and as it turned out, neither did my mother. The whole ritual of dressing up and going from door to door with other children—children I really was not getting along with in the public school, with my rudimentary English and my strange clothes—made me feel there was something a little off, a sinister side to these smiling, ever-cheerful Americans. I told my mother I did not want to go out and she understood.

My father said he had to go out, that there was a faculty party he had little choice but to attend, if he wanted to extend his sessional position past the two semesters. I could tell, from the way my mother nodded into her plate of egg noodles and cheap steak coated in paprika ("American budget dinner!"), that she could sense he wasn't telling the truth.

After it got dark, children started coming to our door. My mother, perhaps frightened that these Americans might get us sent back if they thought we were unfriendly, first gave them all our apples from a bag she had bought at the discount grocer. Many were small, bruised and sour, and the children did not conceal their displeasure. She then doled out small bunches of little purple grapes my father took in his lunches, but they were soon gone, and all that was left was a bar of the dark and bitter chocolate that she used for making frosting for tortes. One little girl tasted a square and spat it out right on our doorstep. My mother smiled at the girl's father, but once she had shut the door she cursed under her breath.

She then went into the pockets of one of my father's jackets, looking for the mints he had begun to eat compulsively while he tried to quit smoking. Instead, she found a note. She read it closely, as if she was decoding a secret message, over the light in the kitchen. She grunted, a strange kind of animal sound, and then ripped up the note into the tiniest of pieces. She yanked open one of the kitchen drawers and rifled through it until she had found what she needed—a paper lunch bag. She picked up a pair of scissors from another drawer like a dagger, still grunting, and made two holes in the bag, laughed to herself and then ran to me. She tugged me by the arm and led me to the front door closet, told me to put on my shoes. We were going out and we had to borrow Bonnie's car.

I had no idea who Bonnie was, but evidently she and my mother knew each other well enough. She lived in the bungalow two doors down, and I'm sure I would have recognized her on the sidewalk. But when she stood on the other side of a screen door, a heavy, shadowy figure in a housecoat, her hair a sickly, peroxided yellow, she embodied all the strangeness of Americans, and I felt a twinge of anger at my mother for being so familiar with the enemy. My mother lied to Bonnie, I could hear that much, she said I had swallowed Pine Sol and that she needed to take me to the hospital. Bonnie nodded, and silently handed my mother a set of keys.

We got into a black Ford Valiant. I remember the name of the car because I had seen the word on a comic. The prince with the funny haircut. My mother pulled out a road map from the glove compartment, mouthed some street names to herself, and ran her finger along a route. She told me not to say a word, she was very upset.

She drove recklessly and faster than my father ever did. She had a clear sense of where we were going now and was more confident and assured than I had ever seen her, muttering to herself. She hated him, she hated this country, and she wasn't going to let me become an American whore.

With the streetlights glowing like a line of little full moons, she slowed down to read house numbers. She pulled up to a red brick bungalow with the curtains drawn, no candlelit pumpkin, the number 28 barely legible under the light near the mailbox, and cut the engine.

She breathed deeply and let out a small sigh. Then she pulled out the paper bag from her purse. I could now see that the holes in the bag were slits for eyes. She gently fitted it over the crown of my head, my ears. Once I could see again through the slits, it was her tear stained face I saw.

"I want you to go to that door. Knock on it. Someone will come. I want you to say trick or treat."

And so I did, precisely as she instructed. The person who came to the door was, I found out later, a woman who was a film professor. She saw my mother sitting in the Valiant. She brought her hand up to her mouth. And then she called my father to the door.

He came, grinning as if expecting a friendly surprise, doing up the rhinestone buttons on his new cowboy shirt. He looked at me wearing the paper bag over my head, my mother in the car, and his smile evaporated. All I remember from the rest of the evening was a screeching, bawling argument in that woman's front yard.

We returned home at Christmas time, and we never went back to America. My mother began to change soon after. I first noticed it in the way she dressed: much more conservatively, no more bright clothes. My father seemed to take the change with an air of resignation. I think he tried not to notice her newfound interest in politics and her clipped way of talking. It was as if he blamed himself for the transformation. He withdrew into himself, with a gentler way about him, but he also began to drink more, and he cared less about his appearance. I think he barely hung on to his instructor's position. They began to drift apart.

My father became more dependent on his drinking to get through each day while my mother got more religious, rediscovering her roots as she escaped into her work with the Muhamed Hevaji cultural foundation. Things got worse when my father lost his position teaching at a college for film studies and could only find part-time shifts as a security guard at the Sarajevo Museum. Though my mother would not say anything negative about him to me, I could sense her shutting him out of her life. She was keeping very busy, doing more translation work than ever before, and had accepted a promotion with the foundation, knowing full well it would keep her away from the apartment for more hours each day. She had taken to wearing a headscarf and would not allow my father to have alcohol in the house. And so he would stay out late drinking through the family savings at the Brigand, his favourite bar in Baščaršija, at least three or four times a week. If we were all at home together for any more than a couple of hours, as sometimes happened on a Sunday afternoon, a loud argument was inevitable. It was obvious that they were only staying together because, in my mother's embrace of Islam, she would not even think of divorcing, though she had told him it was also for the sake of my upbringing. I was oblivious to the political conflict that was about to tear Sarajevo apart because I was dealing with all the drama of the fragile detente at home, helpless and angry that I was in some way responsible for my parents' unhappiness.

It was around this time that my father, with too much free time on his hands, retreated from the world to be closer with his first love, what he called his "Russians"—his translations of Gogol, Chekhov, Dostoevsky, Lermontov and Leskov—and his books of philosophy, their pages underlined and ringed from coffee cups, stacked like old bibles on one shelf. In the mornings, even with the drinking, he was up before everyone else, scribbling away in the little black books he kept on the preserve shelf near the kitchen. Though he wouldn't show anyone what he was writing, I think it was an overt gesture to reconnect with my mother, to show he was still in touch with that part of him she fell in love with: the quiet, charming man who had a sly sense of humour and wore his literary leanings lightly.

He was disciplined with his time. At seven-thirty precisely he would begin preparing our breakfast, seeing me off in the mornings, while my mother was often rushing off to catch a bus to her office, pausing only to scold me for the state of my clothes, my hair, expressing her disappointment with me in one way or another. Despite my father's ambitions for a career in filmmaking and then his refuge in academia both coming to nothing, I did not see him as the failure my mother did. He seemed more at peace with the world, as if he was coming into the life he should have been living all along.

My mother was lost to him by then, though. She treated those notebooks, his Russians, and the books of his favourite philosophers—Wittgenstein, Cioran, Epictetus—as if they didn't exist; not once did she even glance at his notebooks. Perhaps she could never forgive him for how he had betrayed her in America.

How selective she was with her memory, and to her own advantage. As I remembered it, she was far from innocent when it came to infidelity. She recast that time in her life as a moment when she was corrupted by influences she could neither control nor truly understand, so insidious were they. To her, my father was a living example of someone suffering from the diseases of the new corruption, and he had taken me with him on his journey away from faith.

I was happy to go with him in that direction.

As much as I wanted to understand my father's secret world of books and writing, I did not have the attention span or the interest for literature myself. Too many people I loathed—my history and literature teachers, the football-playing boyfriend of the biggest bitch in my class (who was also a snitch about smoking and drinking on school property)—spoke about how they had read *Demons* and *Dead Souls*, how these books were still so timely. As far as I was concerned, from the forty or so pages I had read of Dostoevsky's *Demons*, they offered nothing of interest about the world I was living in. If one of those Russians had written a dark parody that depicted what was happening in my country, then maybe I would have read a few pages out of admiration for the writer's courage.

With my father's books of philosophy, it was a little different. One in particular I could not resist: *A Short History of Decay*. A few pages in, I loved the voice of the author. So contrary, and so theatrical with its learned pessimism. I found the same kind of voice in *Beyond Good and Evil*, in the maxims and arrows. This was a kind of writing as performance, with the voice strong, upfront, so present on the page.

I tried to discuss these with my father, and I was surprised that he did not really care for my newfound enthusiasm. He told me it was dangerous to read these books so young, and that it was even worse with the Greeks. I would think I knew more than I really did, because they only seemed so clear and simple. "You should start with something more contemporary, more scientific." He gave me a translated essay by an American named Nagel, called "What Is It Like to Be a Bat?"

"You should start thinking about reflection itself, little one," he said, "the limits of what we can know. It will make you less arrogant and superficial."

I would have none of it, of course. I read the essay but I found it almost impenetrable. The author's argument seemed to be that we could never imagine how a bat perceives the world, because its sonar receptivity was so profoundly alien. And with this central truth there was evidence of how limited our understanding of consciousness really was. We could only think our way into the inner world of other humans at best, but even that road was full of many wrong turns, my father said. I told him he sounded like he was frustrated trying to understand my mother, but he didn't even smile.

"Literature is flawed by design, but I go to it for its noble failing," he said. He said the most beautiful poem he had ever read was Wittgenstein's *Tractatus*. He could never write something that beautiful, even though there was virtue in trying, and he could never write literature like the Russians either. What remained were what he called his little plays, which he described as comedies of our profound misunderstandings.

I asked if I could read any of his work, and he refused. "Some day when you're older, okay? You want to see a real play, you should go see something Milan is doing."

I imagine he spoke to my mother about our conversation soon after, and they came to an agreement about this educational experience. It was only a couple of days later that he came home with tickets for the show my Uncle Milan was directing, a production of Ionesco's *The Chairs*. He had spoken to him and Milan had said he would be happy to have me as his guest for a premiere performance.

At first I was deeply skeptical, compliant rather than in any way enthusiastic, but off I went. Milan met me at the front entrance of the theatre. He was much more slender then, with a few strands of grey in his unruly dark hair. He looked more like some bumpkin who had just come to the city than one of the country's best directors. He shook my hand like I was a little boy and told me how pleased he was that I was taking an interest.

Once he had taken me to my seat like an usher not quite sure of his job he excused himself, mumbling that he was still needed backstage. I sat there in the dark, moments before the curtain rose, pondering the possibility of making a quick exit.

But then the lights came up. I still remember the set design so vividly—all the props so white and fake looking, the backdrops seeming like some madman had hurriedly made sketches of a family home on Japanese screens. The actors playing the old husband and wife came on, declaiming in that strange, nonsense dialogue, like an English language lesson in one of those Russian videos they made us watch in grade school, and there was a sense of desperation in the characters that I found riveting. The marriage was coming apart under the surface of all the banality. When the two characters committed suicide at the end, I laughed in the dark, even though I knew I sounded hysterical, to conceal that I was actually crying.

I walked home alone from the theatre that night and I felt I had experienced an epiphany. I remember that I wrote about it in my diary by the weak glow of a flashlight, declaring that my destiny had been revealed: "I was born for a life in the theatre." I resolved to try out for the national school and in the meantime find any and every opportunity to act.

My first step was to call Uncle Milan. I made an idiot of myself praising the actors, the set design, the stark, uncompromising vision he had created. When I think about it now, here I was, rebelling against my mother's newfound piety and religious conviction and yet I was behaving like a true believer in the church of what I thought was the highest art form. I know I must have made Milan slightly uncomfortable. I'm sure I sounded like the most stage-struck innocent. He was polite and kind enough to indulge me, suggesting I should audition for a play at my high school that his old friend, my history teacher Ms. Barić, was directing. All these years later, I am still embarrassed by how I squealed in delight in response.

The play was Chekhov's *The Three Sisters*. As soon as I saw the title on the notice I went to the library and read the play in one sitting. I was so intensely focused on each page; it was like a puzzle I had to solve. I knew virtually nothing about Chekhov, never mind the world of the characters in the play, but after the first act I could close my eyes, picture Irina, Masha, Natasha. The male characters by comparison were a little vague to me; when I closed my eyes I saw bearded, costumed approximations of American actors from the badly dubbed nighttime dramas that were the latest thing on TV. And though I could sense the outline of Chekhov's plot from act to act, I couldn't understand the deeper logic.

Now I know that reading a play like a real actor is similar to how a musician listens to a symphony, but at that time, in comparison, the characters were pop songs on the radio to me. With the women, each one was a power ballad. Masha was the song I wanted to learn how to play.

So I went to work at it. I practised and practised my audition piece, a speech by Rosalind in Shakespeare's *As You Like It*, taken from a book I found in the library. I had never read Shakespeare, never mind the play, but once I had memorized the words, I put together a collection of gestures and worked on my voice enough to believe I looked and sounded like the actresses in the dubbed Shakespeare movies on TV. I knew what I had come up with as a performance was a long way from Milan's production of *The Chairs*, but it was a start, and it took all my courage to get through without shrivelling up and crying, afraid I was not worthy of what I desired most in the world.

True to my worst fear, it was at the audition that I discovered that life, no matter what we do, is not fair. We are not all created equal. Some of us can work hard and never be rewarded, and others, with hardly any effort, can come in and snatch the prize, on the strength of a mysterious quality within them. A girl I barely knew, Dragana Markečić, provided me with this lesson.

Within seconds of seeing her onstage, anyone could tell she was blessed, and she could make a career of this work if she wanted to. I immediately hated her for her long blonde hair, her almond-shaped eyes, the music in her voice. She was about five kilos overweight but she carried it so well. She was the first woman of my age in high school who could have been considered voluptuous. Some months later she would become in many ways the sister I always wished I had, but in that moment, seeing her on that stage in that audition, all I could feel was rage at her gift, the ease in which she claimed everyone's attention.

When the results of the auditions were posted on the bulletin board by the auditorium, I was saved from complete despair, though. I had won the part of Irina, the youngest sister, while Dragana had taken the prize role of Masha, the one with all the wit, humour, and life. I told myself I was too homely to carry a bigger role. I was flat-chested, with a boy's hips and even a downy little moustache (but only my mother was aware of this, thank God, and allowed me to go to the aesthetics studio by the train station to have it removed every few weeks). But if I couldn't be beautiful I would impress by my passion.

During those rehearsals I discovered I was incapable of hating Dragana. She was too warm, too generous of spirit, too funny, with a vulgar, sexy way with words that seemed far beyond her years—so far, in fact, that when she joked to me that she had spent a summer sleeping with men a decade older than her while living near the naval base in Split, I found it hard not to believe her (it turned out it was all the influence of her father's mistress, according to her). She made me laugh both on and offstage, especially on our walks home, late in the evening. She also showed me the knife she carried in her purse, a habit she had picked up in Split, and it was around that time that I began to carry my own. I think of her now as the person who really taught me how to be a woman, though it was far from the kind of woman my mother hoped I would become.

My mother sensed Dragana's influence on me immediately. She was not the most attentive of parents, but if there was one area of my life she attempted to control with an impressive commitment to surveillance, it was my sex life. If I stayed out past six on a school night, aside from when I was rehearsing, she needed to know who I was with, and made sure that my father would pick me up. If he protested at all, he faced her wrath; she would accuse him of permitting his own daughter to become the kind of slut he liked to screw back in America. The result was that I remained a virgin until we had to leave Sarajevo, and during this time I only went out on a handful of dates with a boy named Dušan Filipović, who played Andrey in *The Three Sisters*. I stopped seeing him when he broke out with bad acne, an affliction that he said was caused from the cold cream we used during the play.

Poor Andrey, but at least he could say there was some lasting effect on his life from the show. After the final night of the production I went back to my miserable old self in many ways, though I suppose I had become a bit more bookish. I had resolved to read everything Chekhov had ever written. Just in the conversation my acting studies had created with my father, some good came of my mediocre stage debut. As I tried to rekindle all the excitement in my life from my time on stage, there were many days I wondered if I would ever get the chance to be up there again.

What was it like to be a bat, indeed? I felt I was living in a cave, picking up signs of life in the dark with a faint sense of echolocation. My little wings couldn't take me anywhere.

The real change in my fortune occurred when Dragana and I got part-time jobs at the Café Janus, an old haunt of actors, directors, and playwrights, a tavern made over decades before to look like the Deux Magots in Paris, with gingham tablecloths and black and white eight-by-tens of the regulars over the years. It was run by a couple, Aldin and Marija, who had once had careers onstage themselves. The two of them were generally easy to get along with, as long as they weren't going through one of their periods of loathing each other. Dragana once joked that they should meet my parents, that would snap them out of it. The Janus was about three doors down from the Brigand, so I felt that, because of the proximity, my father approved of me waitressing. I knew my mother wouldn't, and, sure enough, two nights into my first week of shifts, she said a blouse I wore to work made me look like a slut. I didn't care. I wasn't dressing for her, or for any of the male customers either. I was dressing for Dragana, who I still believe got me the job.

The more I look back on our time together then, the more I come to the conclusion that I was actually in love with Dragana. Here she was, talented and attractive enough to have gotten a professional football player for a boyfriend if she had wanted, and to have found herself a talent agent who would have inevitably found her work on some ridiculous variety show on TV, and then a bit part on a daytime drama, and then a few choice speaking roles in movies, and then on to what passed for trashy celebrity status in our country before the war. It was a familiar enough career track, one that depressed me as I realized it was the pinnacle of success for young women working in the theatre. And yet Dragana did not seem interested in all of that. She was saving money and studying English and German at the cheap Berlitz rip-off school three afternoons a week. She encouraged me to study with her as well, because there was only one real way of realizing better dreams for ourselves, she said: we had to get to Berlin. Her plan was that we would get an apartment together and find work in a real theatre community, one that was a part of the good Europe, not the one we were doomed to live in for the rest of our lives if we settled for what our fucked up little country, soon to be destroyed, was offering us. Over a glass of horrible Romanian wine in the Janus, an hour after closing one night, she put it all plainly to me: was I in? I don't think I have ever loved anybody as much as I loved her then. She was giving me a plan, and she offered herself to me as an ally in the battle, she said quite seriously, for our souls.

Perhaps it is a failing of my character that I have never loved the right people. I have always loved the ones who have given me the most hope to escape my unhappiness. It might explain why I can play my role so effectively with Dejan. His jealousy is a tribute to my performance.

I have spent years thinking of myself as a kind of crazy woman, but I feel sane and a little more human by finding a way to explain myself here. I feel brave enough to give myself the truth.

I was learning to become a waitress (and a good one, if I do say so myself) serving the theatre people who came in most nights after their performances. According to Milan this was also the period when he and my father, out of their late-night conversations at the Brigand, concocted the plot of a political satire. Called *The (Black) Blood Of A Poet*, (all echoes of Cocteau's work were no doubt intentional), the work would dramatize the rise of a ridiculous figure, a failed psychoanalyst and terrible poet, to a position of great political power in an imaginary country where everyone, as the narrator says in the piece, "had gone a little cuckoo from the waterborne disease of nationalisamilius." My father wrote the first draft in those mornings before he headed off to work. The pages he brought in a notebook to the Brigand in the evenings had the makings, Milan was convinced, of one of the best plays ever written in what used to be our country.

Perhaps it really could have been that strong a work; there was no way my mother and I would have ever known. My father kept his play a secret in our house. Over the years I have speculated on why this was. There might have been an unflattering female character in the early drafts, based on my mother. Or maybe he knew she would be enraged by the risk he was taking, with our welfare as well as his. Because, as Milan told me, it certainly did not take a genius to see that the poet who rises to political prominence was obviously meant to be the man who still remains a fugitive in my broken little country, with so much blood on his hands.

And yet, all these years later, I still wonder if it all happened as Milan described it. I mean, if it was a play my father and he decided to work on together over drinks, the Brigand was hardly a place with the kind of atmosphere where the conversation lent itself to such plans. It had always been a little rougher, frequented by bus and train drivers, and shift workers in the few smaller factories near that part of town. The music from the ancient jukebox was always too loud, as I remember it, blaring some of the worst Serbian pop songs. The beer and wine were cheap, befitting the customers and certainly befitting my father's security-guard's budget. Everybody knew it was common to go in for a drink later in the night and find yourself in the middle of a melee over an argument about football or, increasingly, politics. When I had asked Milan why they had chosen such a place to launch their plans for my father's play, he told me it was precisely because of the atmosphere, and the lack of intimidation my father felt among the workers rather than the *artistes*, as he said. He still had a lot of that old socialist baggage. Neither of them cared about a cultured audience, Milan said. That might have been true, given how disillusioned my father had become with those he called professional intellectuals—people like my mother.

To Milan's credit, he was wise about the risks that being involved with any kind of production would have created for me. He knew I would have been grateful to help out in any capacity, given what little luck I was having in my auditions for small productions and in finding an agent for television work after the school production of *The Three Sisters* completed its two-week run. He also understood that things were getting very strange, the more you paid attention to what was happening in the real world.

It seemed new political parties formed every week, all mysteriously well funded, with ads on the radio and TV. And with these parties, apparatchik types had re-emerged, like stock characters from the dark comedy of life before the Berlin Wall crumbled. War characters.

These men, mostly my father's age, had suddenly been spotted in attendance at the smaller playhouses. They were taking notes, people said at the Janus. Dragana had told me of an old comedian, hired as an MC at an auto show (where she had a weekend job doing nothing more than being photographed lying on the hood of a Dacia, she said) who had made a few quips about Slobodan Milošević while onstage, and who was jumped by three men while walking back to his hotel. He was beaten so badly he had to be hospitalized. Perhaps those goons at the auto show had taken it upon themselves to teach the old man a lesson, as they told the comedian in the moments before he lost consciousness. More than likely somebody had given that order, some mediocrity who, a few weeks before, had been a union steward or low-ranking bureaucrat, and who was now dressed in a better suit and carried business cards with a party logo. In the chatter at the tables most nights at the Janus, I could make out that such incidents like the one at the auto show were occurring more and more frequently, but, little fool that I was, I presumed the artists I served beer and wine to would remain impervious to all of that.

Yet no one was going to be sheltered for much longer; the murder of Asim Žalica, my mother's boss and the director of the foundation, made that clear. It happened late on a Friday afternoon, as Žalica was leaving Gazi Husrev-bey Mosque. He was speaking to two old men before he was attacked, one a professor of philology who had students who came into the Janus regularly. A table of them, who had come from visiting their professor at the hospital, told us about it: a white van had pulled up, and two young men got out, both dressed like they were going to watch a football match rather than to slash an old man's throat. They moved quickly; they knew exactly who they were looking for. The larger one of the two provided the muscle to clear the way, and the slender one, who could only be identified by his floppy blonde hair and blue warm-up jacket, pulled out a switchblade and with one quick stroke ended Žalica's life. The blood poured from Žalica's neck on the cobblestones like a lamb bled before the spit.

Žalica, a friendly bear of a man with John Lennon glasses, had appeared before committee in parliament two weeks before, speaking on interfaith initiatives. He had ridiculed some sycophant of Milošević's who had tried to bully him into denouncing his Orthodox Christian colleagues at a conference Žalica had attended. The whole incident did not even merit a couple of lines in the newspapers, but somebody was taking notes, maybe the same person issuing the orders to young men in white vans.

Police claimed to be investigating, but no one actually believed Žalica's murderer would ever be found, let alone arrested and tried. That is how jaded even students from my school had become about murders on the street, after just a few months of political unrest.

Žalica's death was decisive for my mother. She had become close to him, apparently, seeing in him a kind of hippie wisdom and humility that had come from a thoughtful embrace of faith in mid-life—an embrace much like her own, she said. When she read the newspaper story of his murder on the Saturday morning, weeping at the kitchen table, I had to wonder, given how broken she seemed, whether there was anything romantic between them. It only heightened my suspicions when I saw how sternly she rejected my father's efforts at comforting her as well. She hurried off to the foundation that morning and, when she returned, at about nine in the evening, she announced to my father that she was leaving Sarajevo for Foča at the end of the month, and that she was going to take me as well. She put it plainly to my father: he could join her there or he could decide to stay in Sarajevo, but if he chose the latter she did not want to see him ever again.

It was during this conversation that my mother found out about my father's theatre project with Milan. He called it that; he couldn't quite get the words *the play I have written* out of his mouth. He was explaining to her that he had more commitments in Sarajevo than simply contributing to the rent as best as he could and sharing the responsibility of raising me. As far as I was concerned, both he and my mother could relieve themselves of any further responsibilities to me and I would only be happier, but I kept my mouth shut. That was their argument. It was his opportunity to justify who he had become over the last few years, to proclaim that he was not so dissolute, aimless and—an important point to note for my mother—faithless, as she presumed. He had an inner life, he told her; she was not the only serious person under our roof. Sarajevo had been his home since he was four years old and now, more than ever, he felt it was important to be courageous. It was necessary to take a stand and not let those who were making names for themselves by trading in the politics of fear debase and destroy the foundations of what could be, for the first time in decades, a legitimate democracy. This act of resistance was not just for the city but for the whole of Yugoslavia. He gestured to me as if I were their house pet. "Don't think of me, think of what running from Sarajevo says to Nataša about what is important in life."

I think of my mother's response now, all these years later, and consider it the moment their marriage truly came to an end. At first she smiled, but it was a grin of condescension, even contempt. All of this was surprising, she said, coming from a man who had once bragged he hadn't voted for over a decade, and that even then it had only been to keep his job in the university in Mostar, one of the few places he had happily chosen to live to get away from Sarajevo. She was glad to hear that some use had come from his drinking at the Brigand. How wonderful that it had resulted in a skit, penned with help from one of the few friends who could still tolerate him. Yes, all of it had amounted to a welcome revelation, she was pleased to hear he had finally found his true calling as a barstool comedian quick with a high-toned quote that betrayed his literary credentials. Like the true Marxist he had once claimed to be, he had to acknowledge that the primary consideration for all of life's decisions was economic. She had signed the lease to our home, she had been paying all the bills and seventy percent of the rent for more than two years. And because I was still by law considered a child, she was taking me with her. If he chose to stay in Sarajevo, that was fine with her, but he would be broke and homeless, a tramp with a menial job and a trunk of old books.

Sometimes, I think now, it was not the Bosnian Serb Army (or the BSA, as we called it) who had marched through Foča and killed my father. No, it was during this argument at the kitchen table that he had truly begun to die. His dignity, his pride and, what's worse, his faint hope that he could possibly win back my mother's love were so deeply wounded by her triumphant smile, her silence, her business-like march into the bedroom they shared.

He wasn't going to let the wound go as deeply as was intended without summoning his own defences. He rose from his chair and declared that at least he was still true to his own friends. He did not try to escape his past by throwing himself into religion and working for a foundation that did less for the community it served than for its well-paid staff and board of directors.

She laughed under her breath. It was a cackle, a most unattractive sound, which she made when she was angry with him. She looked down at the floor and squinted in a performance of serious contemplation. And then she calmly began to speak once more. "I am so glad you and Milan have become such friends over the years. Even though I'm sure it can never make up for how he slept with me behind your back, I am happy to see how you've found in such a man a true companion and collaborator."

I only remember my father struggling to laugh, and sputtering. "What are you talking about?" But she had already turned her back on him and was walking down the hall. Then we both listened to the sound of her removing her clothes from the dresser and placing them on their bed. My father followed her down the hall then shut the door, but whatever was said between them did nothing to stop her packing her things. She ordered me to have mine packed by the morning.

She was gone that night, sleeping at a colleague's house, she said, and it was a long five days later before she would come to the café for me. When she did appear she was driving a rented car, a yellow Fiat she said would get us to Foča. We were going to take the journey with a German friend of hers, Irmgard, who waved from the passenger side out there on the street. Who was Irmgard, with her frizzy hair and a gap between her two front teeth? I never really did find out either, though there was some mention of her being a journalist working on a book about the foundation. She was just another mysterious part of my mother's secret life, one that now took us both away from Sarajevo, far from my father, Dragana and the Janus café, from all I had come to love as my home.

My father did follow us to Foča about a month later, but he would not talk about his final days in Sarajevo when he arrived. He had his eyes on the present rather than the past, he said. "And our present—and future—is Foča, Button." Button was his pet name for me, but that is another story. As was my life in Foča, of course.

And it will now have to wait. I have been in this restaurant and really, it has the best name for what I have been doing here for the last two hours: Yesterdays. When you look around here, at the four Korean tourists in spotless, identical tennis shoes, at the two locals examining some legal document, everyone in here looks as though yesterday was their best moment. No one looks under sixty. Though the place is not exactly busy, the waitress and the man in kitchen whites who looks to be the owner have been looking at me funny for the last half hour or so. In all the time I have spent here, all I have had is an English muffin and four and a half cups of coffee. I am taking advantage of everyone's hospitality, testing their patience. If spending time in this country has given me anything, it has taught me when it's time to leave.

19. Lucien Bollinger

It was my last night of classes before I was headed to Montreal. There was no word from the police that they were any closer to finding Nataša. It seemed the logical place she would return to, given how dangerous it might be for her in Toronto. That was me hoping for the best, of course, not allowing myself to entertain the notion that she had been abducted. As I walked out of the doors of the Parkdale school and said my goodnights to the students, I felt liberated, finally acting rather than reflecting.

As I approached the front of my building I could already feel something was wrong. The front hallway light was off. No one on my floor would do that. Timo, the building manager, walked each new tenant through what he called "safety importance thinking." It felt too quiet as I walked down the hall to my door. I turned the knob and it was already open. My sudden concern over the few things I owned overrode any thought I had about my own safety, and I walked in.

I heard the click of heels on the wood of my desk. I flicked on the light. There was a man, feet up, leaning back in my chair, grinning.

Well what can I tell you about him? He was small but wiry and powerful-looking. Hair so blonde I'm guessing it was a dye job. Hooded jersey, baggy pants, I mean, he looked like a hundred guys in my neighbourhood except for that glare, the sculpted look to his face that suggested his whole body was cut for battle. He had the big kitchen knife I had brought back from Japan in his hands.

"Lucien. What kind of name is that?"

"It's French."

"You French?"

"No."

He let out a hoarse giggle. "What, your mother fuck some French guy then?"

"Who are you?"

"You don't worry about who I am, motherfucker. I'm the one asking the questions."

I recoiled, took a step back. That was a bad idea. He pointed the blade at me.

"And don't you fucking move." He rose from the chair and approached me, smiling. He was delighted by my fear. "I read your emails here. I did my own investigation."

I took a quick look at the other side of the room. It was dimly lit but I could make out that the place had been trashed. My clothes were strewn across the floor, two pillows gutted by the knife.

"So romantic, all your messages to Nataša. Like French lovers, am I right?"

He stuck the tip of the blade on the lapel of my jacket. He smelled like alcohol. Something cheap and very strong.

"I'm going to tell you something I did during the war in my country. I knew this guy was banging a Serbian chick in the town we took. I gave him the blade. There I stood before him, no weapon! I gave him a choice. He could cut off his own dick or I would cut it off for him and stick it in his mouth. It was amazing. This guy, he could have stabbed me right there. You know what he did?"

I could feel my knees quake, the piss start to flow down my leg.

"He cried like a fucking baby and did the job himself. Isn't that crazy?"

He moved the tip of the blade to my fly.

"Crazy but smart though because I let him live. For a while."

A small moan escaped me and amused him. He giggled again.

"You're going to forget about Nataša, okay? She's gone. Understand?"

All I could do was nod and swallow.

"Think of her as dead, okay? That way, you live, you got it?"

He moved the blade away from my fly and reached into his front pocket. He pulled out the keys to my father's car. He trilled, in falsetto, "I have the key to your heart."

"No. Please, that's not my car."

"I'm going to leave you now but you're not going to follow. I'm taking these. Until tomorrow you're not going to go anywhere or call anyone, okay?"

I nodded, glanced over at my phone and saw that the line was cut.

"Here. Give me your cell."

He smiled as I handed it over. Then he threw it on the tiled floor with all the force in him. He stamped on it to finish the job.

"I think we're done now."

He calmly moved away from me and walked over to my desk again. He laid the knife by my laptop and then picked up a plastic gas canister he had placed on the floor. He moved as if he was off to work. Places to go, people to see.

Though he could not resist a parting thought. "I think of your body every night we're not together."

Words I had written to Nataša, some weeks before. He giggled again as he walked by me and out into the night.

The next day, Aquino showed me the grainy black and white video from the parking lot of my building. The guy's hood is up, draped over his face. He moves so quickly and efficiently—I'd say even gracefully—as he pours out all the gasoline from the plastic canister on the hood of the Regal. He stands back, lights a match and a cloud of white flame goes up. I asked Aquino to shut the video off at that point, I didn't have to see any more of it.

20. Milan Zujović

When there are arguments in rehearsal, I can deal with them. I play the diplomat very well. It is another performance—call it meta-theatrical. It is only at home that I fail as a diplomat, at least with Mira.

She is still simmering with rage about two emails I had received and carelessly left open. One was from our young lighting designer for the production, Rebecca. Mira sees it as flirtatious because the young woman raves about what we discussed about Cassandra in rehearsal, all the reading she's now doing to affirm my contention that the character is actually schizophrenic. And why would she be flirtatious unless I would give her reason to think I was open to such overtures? The second was from Nataša. I don't know what Mira could possibly see as enraging about that one, all Nataša said was that she was in Calgary, en route to us here, and that she was thankful I had not told anyone about our correspondence, that she was still scared for her life. Yet Mira was furious. She accused me of trying to seduce Rebecca Rieff and of having unnatural feelings for Nataša. Let me be clear: I have never wanted to seduce Rebecca Rieff and, as for Nataša, I was going to do what I considered the honourable thing and not betray her trust in me.

Mira said she didn't care about such betrayal. She told me I was blinding myself to the truth. Nataša was lying! Well, what can I say? My only response to her was that she had no idea what Nataša had gone through during the war in our country. Mira could not judge.

Bad idea, telling another survivor she can't understand such behaviour, I suppose. But at least it took Mira's mind off Rebecca as she lectured me on Nataša's bad choices and how she loathed my victim talk. "As long as you're alive," she said, "you decide to be a victim or you decide to be a survivor, nobody else makes that decision for you."

I found it hard to believe that Nataša had decided to have people hunting her down. It was a minor point, maybe, but an important one.

I wasn't going to get into it with her, but in the back of my mind was what had happened to Dragana—Dragana Markečić. I knew the girl back in Sarajevo. She had been a good friend of Nataša's. She was a very talented actor, bright and perceptive. By all accounts she became mixed up with gangsters who were running scams to get people out of the country after the war. Was that a bad choice? I would have done the same thing in her shoes. The girl felt she had no other option, I'm sure. Dragana ended up dead in London.

Bad example, maybe. Mira said it confirmed that I should be talking to the police in Nataša's case. My complicity was unconscionable.

Maybe that was true, but I had my own plan. An old associate of ours back home had gone into government, working for the ministry of culture. He'd done well—far better than he had running a theatre company—and was part of the cabinet. If Nataša was indeed being pursued by war criminals, as she told me in her emails, I knew Zoran could pull the right strings, make sure Interpol and the ICC were on it, and bring these men to justice.

I told all this to Mira but she was skeptical, of course. She called me deluded about my own influence. "Why do you feel so responsible for this girl's safety?" It was a good question, one I really can't answer—at least not to her. I promised her I would go to the police the minute I knew Nataša was in Vancouver.

And truly, I had every intention of doing just that.

21. Nataša Ružić: Notebook Two

Deep dark night at last. It has come down and finally everyone on the bus—the kid with his video game, the two teenage girls with all the drama of their high school romances to discuss between sips of vodka from a flask—has finally gone to slleep and I can write. For the last hour I have been looking out of my window in silence with the video camera cradled in the palm of my hand, recording the view. I watched the night swallow all the contours of the huge line of mountains over the horizon. Night can take in everything but the screaming thoughts in my head.

I need some escape from the situation with Dejan. There I was outside a Chinese restaurant last night, shouting into a payphone. I had called him precisely at the time we had decided upon and his first words to me were accusations: I was a whore who was using him, I deserved to "go down like Dragana." That only enraged me and it got worse.

He found out about Lucien; he discovered him at Alex's funeral. And worse, he tells me he has made sure Lucien won't be writing me any time soon. Of course he didn't believe me when I said I had had no contact at all with him. No, I was probably fucking him for money, like everyone else who's ever shared my bed.

I don't know why I didn't respond better. I haven't been so furious with someone in years. I actually didn't think I was capable of such feelings anymore. Did I feel within me that there was some truth to his accusations, that I am capable of nothing but transactions?

But I swear, that was not why I contacted Dejan again. I consider him as much a victim as I am. I really do want to offer him a chance at making his life over, as much as I want it for myself.

We couldn't have predicted Alex would have come home when he did. Because of the blackout that day he had no sources of light in the house to create the effects he needed, so when he said he was going out to find a patio in Kensington Market I assumed he would be drinking hard again. There were never half-measures with Alex. It all went wrong, but when I tell Dejan I am determined to ensure we both can be free, we can start new lives—together or not—I mean it.

I suppose I am not sure if I have ever believed we can start new lives as some kind of couple. He said it himself, he got his reward that first night we slept together, before I left Toronto. Who's the one who views our being together as a transaction, then?

I don't know how to solve this. If we do things right and get the money from Petar, Milan is the only one who will ever have to know I went through all this. He'll have the clip, and if Petar or Nikola ever try to come for me, he'll know what to do. It can all still work. But now, given what Dejan says he has done to Lucien, who knows how close they are to tracking him down? Every hour he's in Toronto, trying to get this deal done with Alex's paintings, feels like borrowed time. It's a mess.

And Lucien, the dear man. There was no way I could have known I would discover that video clip. There was no way I could have known about Alex's secret paintings when I came to Toronto. I was an innocent . . . Well, as much as I could have ever been an innocent with anyone. It doesn't seem like weeks ago now, it seems like years. If my breaking it off with him wasn't thinking for others and not myself, I don't know what true selflessness is.

I remember talking endlessly with Lucien during the annoying phase of our relationship when he had felt it was his job to fix me. I did not become "vulnerable" with him because I was "opening up" and "learning to trust." I relented and told him what happened to my parents and what I had endured because he was demanding more intimacy than I'm capable of, and lying about it would have taken more energy and imagination, more of a performance, than I had in me. I remain an actress without talent or dedication. There is no fixing what cannot be unbroken.

There once was a Nataša who returned to Sarajevo, so full of ambition, who still believed she could save herself after living through what had happened in Foča.

It was my Uncle Milan who managed to get me back into the city. The war had been good for him. His productions had become, by high-ranking government consensus, the kind of art that met with official approval. In Britain and America the critics loved his opera and theatre productions. In *The Guardian* a critic had praised his *Antigone* and *Macbeth*, both staged in contemporary settings, as "powerful allegories that help a nation to heal." Milan had made work of such impeccable taste it evaded the direct criticism of those in power. Tragedy and suffering were made beautiful and eternal. With his newfound lapdog status he pulled some strings and got me out of Foča. He wrote to say he might have found me work in a theatre production.

His project, which was the accepted term for any initiative sanctioned by the development community and our new bureaucratic overlords, ticked all the boxes for those who imagined our city could be revived and remade as a Euro-capital. It was culture that promoted democracy, they crowed, employed Croats and Bosnians and allowed a heritage building to get capital funding. A famous American writer (though I had never heard of her), Antonia Cronin, had initiated it. She had come to Sarajevo for some international writers' conference and decided to stay on. Simply horrified by how Sarajevo had been transformed by the war years, she felt she had to do something for the suffering, courageous citizens. What she considered we all needed, more than anything else, was for her to direct a Thomas Bernhard play called *Ritter, Dene, Voss.* You know it? Of course not, I don't think anybody does but Antonia Cronin's friends and a few Austrians who still teach such work in their universities. The work concerns two sisters, both actresses, and their philosopher brother Ludwig, who in the course of the play comes back home from a mental institution. A return to sanity; how subtle the allegory.

She had approached Milan because she had heard he could help with her casting and provide her with a good translator, tech crew, and an assistant to the director, one whose English was serviceable. The assistant's role was mine if I really wanted it, he had stated in his letter, and I could stay at his place until I was on my feet. I was being given an opportunity to put my trauma behind me and find solace in the humble but noble work of creating culture.

Of course I was grateful for what Milan had done for me, but once we were under the same roof he soon realized I was not the skinny, bookish, and reserved teenager who had left the city. I had lived through too much, I realize now, and I had grown impatient with artistic pretensions and any kind of entitlement. The plan of one month's residence in the posh, three-bedroom apartment he and his actor girlfriend Mira were renting did not go well. Mira was a woman who seemed to take pride in how fully she lived up to that word diva. She criticized me for how much hot water I used for a shower, and how much espresso I drank from her little drum of expensive Italian she brought back from "Mil-ano." One morning I slapped her for the way she was talking to me, and by that evening I was on a friend's couch, never to return to the bedroom she and Milan had so generously set aside for me, with its crisp white sheets that were so heavily starched I swear they scratched my skin.

If this narrative was in any way predictable that friend I stayed with would have been Dragana. That would have been ideal, but an easy rescue from any bad situation is never possible for me, it seems. I ended up staying with our mutual friend Lila, who had been a waitress with us at the Café Janus. Lila was teaching ballet full time, her hopes for dancing with a company taken away by the war. The frail, bird-like little friend I remembered had become tough and wiry, and scorched by divorce. After two nights on the couch I woke up to her stroking my hair, murmuring that she had always had a crush on me. She took my hand and led me into her bedroom. No commitments, no expectations, be in the moment, she told me.

As for Dragana, she had disappeared from Sarajevo. I heard she was still alive, so I paid a visit to her mother, who was living in one small room in her sister's house. Newly widowed and well into middle age, she was unable to find work even as a house cleaner. Reduced circumstances, as we used to call poverty in those days. It was common enough. Dragana's mother made me tea in the filthy kitchen that smelled of bleach and some other toxic chemical. Her small fat hands shook as she smoked, and she could barely contain her contempt for her daughter. She told me that when Dragana had left for England, eight months before, she promised she would send her money from the wages she would be earning as an au pair. No money had ever come and, what was worse, Dragana had stopped writing. When her mother had contacted the au pair agency to find out if anything might be wrong, she was told Dragana had quit after three weeks, repaid the agency her fare and had informed them she was returning to Sarajevo with a ticket purchased from her own savings.

Yet her daughter was not entirely without a conscience. Not long after her mother's conversation with the au pair agency, Dragana finally answered one of her mother's emails, saying she was fine, and that she was still in the UK. She said she regretted not being able to send money yet, but the au pair job was crap and she was now working as a receptionist at a PR firm in London. Her work visa issues would soon be settled, and all would be well with what she called her new start. She had not asked her mother how she was or even provided her with a new address, though, and disappeared back into some mysterious other life in Britain. It was, Dragana's mother said, as if a robot had written the email. I went back to Lila's that night, bringing a bottle of wine and her favourite French cigarettes, Gauloises, as a rent instalment for my affectionate landlord. I told her precious little about the one friend we were sure was going to make it, and make us all proud; I suppose I wanted to keep Dragana for myself.

At that point I had spent about two weeks at Lila's, and though it was not yet uncomfortable, I knew it would be heading in that direction if I couldn't get working and get on my own. Though Lila had said she understood that we weren't in a relationship, she began to get annoyed if I did not tell her where I was each day. She merely expected my companionship each night. I was resolved: as soon as I was working, I would be gone, yet I discovered my theatre job was far from a sure thing, and that I needed to go through an interview process. This was new information, and I suspected my tiff with Mira had something to do with it. I had to sit down with Antonia Cronin herself, and she would determine if I was right for the assistant's position. Underslept, exasperated, and impatient with any diva-like behaviour like Mira's, I realize now there was no way I could have started work in the right frame of mind.

Antonia was a type of complicated American I hadn't met before. The ones I had come to know in Sarajevo were all military in some way or another, young men and women from places that looked as remote and pathetic as Foča in the bent and faded snapshots they kept in their wallets. They had bad teeth and tattoos that had begun to fade and blur even though none of them seemed past thirty, and they were mostly simple to understand, even when they became aggressive and sentimental after too much drinking. Antonia, when she spoke of other Americans in Sarajevo, had nothing but contempt for their vulgarity. She told me she was from Los Angeles, "embarrassingly enough," but had left for New York as soon as she was able, and had never looked back. From what I managed to uncover prior to our meeting, she lived a charmed life there, flitting from writing book reviews, then plays, then novels to writing and directing short films and, most recently, some avant-garde opera libretti. The photos I found of her, from the seventies, suggested she was capable of appearing glamorous and vaguely exotic, with her long auburn curls and grey eyes. The pendant around her neck in those days was of an Egyptian ankh, like my mother had worn back then. When I remarked upon her career in America and all the amazing artists she must have worked with, she was dismissive, telling me Manhattan would soon be a cultural mausoleum. If I visited, I would see streets once full of galleries and performance spaces now transformed into blocks of nothing but little designer boutiques (sounds great to me, I wanted to say). She didn't seem to like much about her country at all, even though it had clearly been far better to her than it had to the other Americans I had met. She dressed down in denim shirts and jeans and in large, spotless white tennis shoes, yet she wore her greying hair tied back in a Hermes scarf and discreetly flashed an antique watch. There was no mistaking her status.

As she asked me questions about my theatre experience and my education, I got the impression she wasn't really listening to my answers. She was taking in how I sat in the chair, how I sipped my coffee, my father's wedding ring—the one piece of him I managed to recover, and which I wore on my right hand. She was looking for any indication that I might know the codes of the elect, those working in Sarajevo out of some higher principle rather than the need to survive. And suddenly, even though I had disliked Antonia from the moment I sat down, I discovered that it was important for me to master her world. I took it as a challenge to appear as if I might be the child of some fallen aristocratic line, not the daughter of a couple of neurotic ex-hippies who had misread the fates. So, in what was probably the performance of my life, I gave her what she was looking for, speaking with all the haughtiness of my mother in her final years, and dredging up the few quotes of my father's beloved Russians to suggest that I might be a little iceberg of sophistication—so much was under the surface, yes, don't mind if I do take one of your Dunhills, as I exhaled through my nose like what's-her-face in some Godard film.

So I got the job. And when word got back to Milan he came to see me at Lila's with a little bottle of Spanish champagne and a rose in a glass of cut crystal. He said I would have made my parents proud. I kissed his cheek (he smelled like rakija), put the rose in the garbage when he left, drained the glass, and gave what was left in the bottle to Lila. We toasted Dragana, wherever she was.

By the third day of the rehearsals for *Ritter, Dene, Voss*, I could tell I was not the only one who could tell that this was going to be a fiasco. The actors, all no doubt suggested to Antonia by Milan, were really too old for their parts and too surly and unfit for the kind of stylized, physical acting Antonia was expecting from them. Expecting, that is, with no rationale for her choices beyond what we all could sense was an attempt to replicate productions of other plays she'd seen in New York. Despite the actors' physical limitations, what they were remarkably adept at was the language of furtive smiles and eyerolls that Antonia never caught. I wished I could have rolled mine too; my English was strong enough to discern that, as we worked on the script, Antonia's accent would subtly shift as she read the lines, as if she were not from Los Angeles or Manhattan at all but from somewhere in England. She had a strange habit of gesticulating as if she were conducting some musical performance, which caused a shouting match between her and Anel Lulić, the nasty drunk who was playing Ludwig (and who stuck his tongue in my mouth when I gave him what I thought was a polite kiss after our drinks the first night of rehearsals). After that eruption, I think Antonia realized she had lost all credibility, and the support of the actors, but instead of attempting to build it back beat by beat with a closer reading of the lines, she decided she was going to show them how each part should be blocked and acted, as if she were working with three stolid, chain-smoking marionettes she had to move around from place to place onstage. She played each role pop-eyed and robotically, reading in a sing-song voice that could have caused the paint to peel off the walls, if it hadn't already been peeling.

By day four I did the unspeakable: I laughed out loud from the orchestra pit as Antonia was scurrying from place to place onstage, acting out two roles at once. She turned on me and let loose a highly concentrated dosage of the hostility that had been building up inside her ever since she had taken up her position as engaged-theatre-artist-in-residence for the good people of Sarajevo.

"Get out! Get out and don't come back!" she screeched from the stage, with one scarecrow arm in its denim sleeve raised as she directed me to the main exit. I could do little but cover my mouth, nod as my last gesture of deference, and hurry out of the building. I had no clue what would become of me but I at least had willed my own escape, for the first time. It would not be the last.

The worst part was that I hadn't even been paid yet, so I couldn't afford to get drunk. The next day I got up early, looking for the address of the au pair agency that had gotten Dragana out of the country. If it was good enough for her, it was good enough for me.

Thinking of it now, I should have had my suspicions about the Dinarica agency from the very beginning. It was run by a fat gangster with a Stalin moustache, perfumed and bursting out of his shiny suit. He looked like an out-of-work TV presenter. Branko confirmed that it would be easy for me to get my work visa and be on a plane within a week, with the flight paid for by the agency; the fare would be taken out of my wages over the first six months. There were hundreds of people trying to leave Sarajevo, living for months in uncertainty, in a purgatory of red tape, and here I was, with the stroke of a pen, on a two-year contract off to London where I would be met by Dinarica clients David and Jennifer Benton at the airport. I would be driven back to Croydon where I would get straight down to the care and feeding of little Corin and Lucy, three and five, who were, I was assured by the Bentons in their letter to me, simply delightful. David, a solicitor, and Jennifer, an executive assistant working for a Labour MP, were incredibly busy people, I was told. They needed a responsible, caring individual with fair-to-good English and excellent attention to detail. How straightforward and manageable it would all be, how lucky I was!

Within a week of receiving their letter I was on a plane, looking out the window as we ascended into the grey clouds from a Sarajevo I have never returned to. Sometimes I think, on a foolish journey to escape myself, that only there could I truly find a home again.

As I write this I am amazed I can still cry. My reserves of self-pity surprise me.

And I think of Lucien, goddamn him. I worry about what Dejan might have done to him, all that he won't tell me because he already fears I'm pulling away from him. There is so much I want to say.

As for Dejan and his jealousy, how I wish I could scream to him that we were never really close to begin with. It is only further cause for self-loathing to think of how I took his broken child's conception of what love might be and made a travesty of it to exact as much revenge as possible on him and his kind. That is the worst of it.

I can't help feeling that it's all going to be over soon anyway, despite my frail belief that we'll actually get money from Mikha for Alex's paintings and finally have the means to disappear into the safety of new identities. If and when that happens I still don't know what I will do with these notebooks. Seal them away for years until I am truly someone new? Then I can read them and be amused rather than saddened by what happened to the young woman I once was. Memory will finally have no power over me and sleep will come so much easier at last.

22. Alex Rebane

Dear M.,

It's 3 a.m. It is hot, noisy, and a little dangerous to be out there on the street. All the kids have left the clubs and what I can hear from my window is the muffled beat of bass and drums as the boys who couldn't get laid drive back home to the suburbs. It's just the meth heads and the runaways on the street with panhandler sunburns, out there scrounging, rubbing up against each other. Fucking, fighting, or frank negotiations. I think you'd like my neighbourhood, it's got a little of how I imagine Rome must have been.

I've been painting since noon yesterday, stopping to get some Thai curry at what must have been midnight, and I've been beating back sleep with the last of some coke from my new dealer. This guy used to be a boxer, he tells me, and he thinks I should paint him "'cause it looks like you do people good." Well, better to do people good than to do good people, I guess.

I'm still trying to get the last of these Nataša paintings done. I want them out of my system now. Her mood has shifted and she's been nothing but a sweetheart here this last couple of days, keeping my studio and my life out of chaos, patiently sitting for me for hours and listening to all my sordid stories, laughing and frowning at all the right moments. I can only imagine what years of hell she has gone through to carry herself with such quiet dignity and elegance.

But I thought we would become closer. I imagined us developing a relationship like Caroline and I have but she doesn't have Caroline's bitchiness or sense of humour. She worries too much about me.

I put it down to timing. I think she's fallen in love with the amanuensis. I say I think because she doesn't really talk about him when we're together, either because she's consenting to be loved or because she thinks I would think less of her for falling prey to such a conventional notion. Or maybe she thinks I would judge her for being involved with a guy I find increasingly irritating, the way he works so hard to sound knowledgeable about painting every time he's over here. Whatever's going on inside her head, it's taken her focus away from me and this work, and I can't lie, she's not that compelling a person to paint for me because of it.

You know I make no apologies for my narcissism, M. I don't think you ever did either.

Here is the curious thing: before she was in love, there were actually more angles to her, more possibilities with her profile, more personae I could explore, one stroke at a time. But now, what's going on within her has reduced what was in potentia, and to paint her is to fix her, pinned like a butterfly. And I don't care for lepidoptery.

I'm sure for you it was much the same. Always looking for the drama first, and then distilling it into a look, a gesture. I'm just not finding it anymore. I've lost her.

But enough. Maybe it is the frustration of the day's work talking. Time to go to bed, a couple of Percodans, attempt the sleep of the unjust. I'll write again soon.

A.

23. Dejan Vidić

My grandmother used to say that if you didn't know if a storm was coming, you didn't deserve the land you farmed. Or something like that. I'm translating badly and she was old. You can smell rain. You can feel the electricity gathering in the air. That is the feeling I had after that painter's funeral, where I wandered around in the periphery, playing the guest that no one can place but no one has the guts to ask to leave—until I couldn't take it anymore and had to act, to do something with my rage at Nataša's betrayal.

So many questions in my head. For ten days straight I woke up in that gulag of a motel asking myself how I had let this woman make me explode my whole life back in London, get on a plane with a bogus Estonian passport and do her bidding. And she was the one who got angry with me when I found out about this Lucien of hers and demanded an answer. Where were my answers?

I'm a terrible liar. Always have been. And now here I was with Petar in town, meeting him in a hotel bar, with the police looking for me, and he decided to come down on me too for not being able to find Nataša and take her out, as we had agreed. I had to sit there, drinking a pissy Canadian beer and manufacture my frustration about how Lucien, her ex-boyfriend, could tell me nothing, and how the cops were useless in finding her. I couldn't look Petar in the eye.

The worst thing for me was that this was little Petar, the one I protected in school when we were kids. Little Petar the mama's boy who couldn't play football for shit, who dressed like a girl, who was the teacher's pet. Even in the army after he had finally filled out, I looked out for him. Now here he was, with his fake rich girlfriend and his fake rich life, and he had the nerve to tell me that he saw no reason to come through with the money for Nataša. If I did my job as we agreed, he said, we wouldn't need it.

But it was not what we agreed! All three of us had settled on a plan where Petar would come up with the money that Nataša was asking for and Nikola, who had the most to lose given his rank back then, would arrange to meet her in a public place and hand it over to her. Then we would have her tracked. I'd wait for my moment, and retrieve the money. And now Petar was trying to change things.

"I don't see why we need the money. You can deal with her without it."

It made no sense. What, was I supposed to wait for Nikola and her to meet in a public place and off her right there? I was the one taking all the risks.

"You should have thought of what you were risking when you did what you did to Alex," he said.

I was trying to stay on script for Nataša, trying to live the lie we had made and play it as the truth.

"Petar, we need that money from Alex's paintings for this. You don't even have to tell Caroline. Once she's agreed to meet him, you send it to Nikola in a bank transfer, it's out of your account for two, maybe three days before I get it back."

There he was, drinking his ridiculous mojito with the ridiculous plastic straw in his mouth as he laughed at me, spit coming out of the tip of the straw. "Are you crazy?" he said. "Mikha's paying for those. We'll be lucky to get half a mil. And Caroline's got to pay her buddy Barany out of that."

I don't know Barany. And I didn't want to know him either. The fewer people I had to run into from this woman's business . . . you should have seen Alex Rebane's funeral! I have seen some types working the door at the Axe but these ones . . . And half a million! I couldn't hide my surprise. Nataša had told me that the painter's fakes would be worth a lot more. And she told me Caroline and Petar would easily have the money she was asking for, she'd seen their books. So I pushed Petar, he could get the money from their joint account.

He only laughed harder. He said they didn't have a joint account and he wasn't about to ask Caroline. There was no way he would reveal any of it to her.

It was that cocktail straw that did it to me. I slapped it out of his mouth and told him if he had destroyed the Foča tape to begin with, none of this would have happened. He had gotten it from an old friend in London and as soon as he had seen a few seconds of it he should have burned it. He had given Nataša the opportunity to do this to us. I was no longer play-acting. I called her a fucking bitch, and I meant it.

I was starting to hate her. Nataša, the shag of my life. You have to understand, working the door back in London, I saw so many chicks on a daily basis. I dated more than a few but she was different. Maybe she had a hold on me because I thought she was mine for a while and then Petar came over from Montreal. I had never lost a woman to him—when we were young I was the one they wanted to shag. And when Nataša emailed me in July, saying she missed me, she missed us . . . I guess I was doomed. Now here I was, in this mess. I suppose you can only really hate the ones who make you feel so much.

And I suppose if I hadn't really hated my life in London, it wouldn't have been so easy for me to sacrifice it all for her.

The thing about that tape too—I never knew she was in Foča. None of us did. When she and I started seeing each other back in London she told me she had been in Sarajevo during the war. Me, Petar, Nikola, none of us were involved in anything she went through, I swear. I've got no reason to lie to you and I'm terrible at it when I try.

I got through the performance with Petar. Maybe because I got a little violent he believed me. We made peace by saying we'd do one more call with Nikola. If he agreed that we'd give Nataša whatever we made from the sale of those paintings with Mikha, that we'd tell her we'd get her more, that would be enough to move our plan into action.

Of course, the plan Nataša and I had, to take that money and never look back, I was starting to believe that was falling apart too. Lies on both sides, and I didn't know which truth I was on. You could say I was right back in my wartime mind.

Except now I might pay for my crimes.

24. Christina Perretti

So it is done; I've completed my play-acting, got the information I needed from Georg Barany. It is exhilarating in the moment to pretend to be someone else. My heart races, in fear of being caught out, and I feel so sharp, poised for attack. But once it's over I always feel exhausted, coming down from the adrenalin high.

I look at one of these business cards I gave Barany and imagine another life. I could have easily become someone like this Fiammetta Capaldi I impersonated with Barany, toiling away for thirty or forty years doing estate law. I would have probably married someone else at the firm, made partner once our kids were in school. It would have been a good, normal way of living. I would have probably quit smoking years ago.

As my father says, only half-joking, "I gave you my useless Catholic guilt." It's a family trait, a martyr complex that started with my grandparents, it seems—the first generation in my family who stopped going to church. My *nonno* became a communist as a kid during the worst of the war years. And she was the one who pushed my father to study law, and then of course that passed on to me, even though I resisted for years, taking art history, because I figured I had my mother the dressmaker's eye for detail. I was determined to become anything, even a schoolteacher, before following my father. But then the study of art was intrinsically political, especially in the eighties when I was at university. Strong opinions drew me where my father said he always knew I'd end up—in his same precinct, working fourteen-hour days, six days a week. My ex-husband Mauro probably put it best: we can't get off the cross so someone else can use the wood.

My father and I have that one fatal trait you need to be a detective. We are obsessives.

Here I am in a city thousands of miles away from home, chasing down the crumbs of a trail that could only lead farther into the woods. But now, with Lucien Bollinger getting beat up, at least the Toronto police have finally woken up and stopped chasing phantoms for their own political ends. The man who attacked Bollinger, given the description, must be somehow associated with Petar Stepanović. I'm waiting for the report of their next interview with him now. I'm not leaving yet; I know there's more to come.

But I understand the argument from my superiors to close the file quickly. There are higher priority cases, and really, because art theft seems more of a sideline for the Russian and Serbian gangsters involved, there is a better chance they will be caught for something else in the months ahead. Like most successful entrepreneurs, they have diversified interests, from drugs to human trafficking to extortion. Usually that is how we can break a fraud and smuggling ring. In the investigation of other crimes, there's that moment when you realize you've stumbled upon a whole network. Then we can pinpoint the locations where the art is stashed and raid as a matter of course over months, sometimes years.

Still, for me it is never about the big picture. I get fixated on one character, someone only tangentially involved, because I know that person is the one who has dropped the crumbs and can lead me to where the treasure is buried.

It is a shame I couldn't have gotten more from Barany. He was cordial when he greeted me in the offices of Ars Longa, what he calls his fine-art restoration and authentication headquarters. Slick with its pot lighting angled just so on the stone walls, the heavy oak crossbeams that span the high ceilings. It would not be out of place back home in Milan, still had the look of its former incarnation, Studio Barany, where Georg exhibited and sold the work of his father, Ferenc. As soon as Barany had taken my fake business card in his small, manicured fingers, he smiled and tried out his few words of Italian on me. His accent sounded almost Calabrian. You can say I am as prejudiced as my father used to be about southerners, but I can't help it, my first thought was that Barany has some good friends in the Mafia.

I had worked on what I thought was a pretty strong pitch for him. "My *nonna* has left me three paintings she got in Moscow fifty years ago," I said.

"Your grandmother was in Moscow?"

"The Communist party in my country sent her. They called it an education delegation."

The best lies, as they say, have the coarsest grain of truth. My *nonno* actually did spend some time in Moscow. I've seen an old photo of him on an airfield in his huge overcoat. When I inherited it at sixteen, it still smelled of harsh Russian tobacco. I love my *nonno*'s crooked smile in that picture. He was trying so hard to be the hardened, gallant internationalist, with a cigarette in his mouth and a Bogart squint in the harsh winter light.

Barany was brusque with me at first.

"Artist?" he barked. "Provenance?" Did he think I was wasting his time? When I told him I had three Maleviches, he gave me a closer look, peering over his reading glasses. His thick grey hair seemed to shoot out a little higher from the crown of his head.

"You have photos of these paintings?"

I reached into my purse, produced the eight-by-tens of the fakes we had found in Lugano. It wasn't long before he ushered me into the back office of Ars Longa. He asked me if I'd like a drink while we spoke more intimately about the work.

I took him up on the glass of Tokaji. He could not conceal how pleased he was when I told him I read about him in *The Herald Tribune*. There had been a story on his work authenticating a Bacon painting allegedly found in a mechanic's garage in Stepney. Barany beamed, but as he rubbed one hand along the barnwood table between us, as if he could polish it, he looked a touch melancholy.

"You can't imagine the resistance I faced from the academic community. Science? Fingerprinting? How dare some tradesman tell us he knows more than we do about what is real and what is fake!"

"But you had the photographs."

"Not just any photographs. It took me years to develop my camera. Spectrographic analysis. When I started working on it, I couldn't believe that no one had tried this before. Fingerprints don't lie."

Oh, but they do, I wanted to say. Plaster casting and replicating a fingerprint from virtually anything an artist once touched— a matchbook, spectacles—can be employed to make a fingerprint suddenly appear on the back or on the edge of a canvas. And of course it was curious that just as Bacon's studio had all been carefully packed up and sent on tour, with all the chaos of the artist's scattered photographs, his brushes still soaking in coffee cans, suddenly, a new Bacon was found, owing to the scientific advancement in authentication Barany boasted about. Once the project to recreate Kazimir Malevich's studio was carried out in Kiev, a whole trove of his work was magically discovered, all authenticated by this Cheshire cat. The Malevich paintings were a bolder, more ambitious con. Even the blockhead cops in Lugano agreed with me: that's why we went with Malevich fakes, to be safe. Yet here was Barany, still untouchable.

I smiled for him, shook my head. I was probably overacting, but men like him, actors themselves, gravitate to outsized gestures, as if you're tacitly paying them respect. "It's unbelievable that they gave you such a hard time of it."

"Ah, not really. These academics and curators, they know they stand on shaky ground when they tell you only they can determine what is real and what is fake. There's a lot of money involved, so naturally they're going to fight like hell to protect their territory. I bring more science and more objective understanding to the process, and for this I am vilified!"

"That's what I heard from my friend who told me about you. I realized we had to meet."

"Your friend. Who is your friend?"

"Caroline Vidler. I was here visiting and she told me I had to see you."

I knew the moment I mentioned Vidler that I had played my hand too soon. I let him get to me. I had felt an urge to puncture that balloon of self-regard he was so jovially inflating as we sat and drank the wine.

"Ah, Caroline. How is she?" He poked his glasses back up the bridge of his nose, crossed his legs and recomposed himself into a courtly formality, as if he had snapped shut his suitcase of baubles and fake watches at the fair. "You know her well?"

After that, it was all bad acting and fabrication on my part. I babbled on about meeting Caroline at the Frieze art fair and made one last attempt at re-establishing that confidential tone the wine had brought on by intimating how much I didn't like her new boyfriend Petar. I got a flicker of recognition, and the beginnings of a grin that suggested he admired the work of another professional liar. From then on, he became formal, speaking in clipped phrases as if he was suddenly struggling with English. He performed a parody of solicitousness.

"I'll tell you what, Ms. . . . Capaldi. Here's my card. Next time you're in Montreal, if you can bring one of your Maleviches, maybe you, me, and Caroline can have dinner and talk about what I can do for you, how is that?"

I told him that would be lovely. I practically fawned. I used to be a much better actor.

And that was that. Perhaps it had less to do with my performance than with Barany's feelings about Caroline Vidler that our conversation ended so abruptly. I would not be surprised if he had fallen out with her. There could be any number of reasons, but the fact that, through Petar Stepanović, Caroline had introduced a dangerous, volatile criminal element into a transactional process that was supposed to remain codified was most probable. It would be worthwhile to pay attention to Barany over the next few days and weeks. That was going to be my recommendation in my report, but I knew no one, not the Montreal police nor my own colleagues with Interpol, would have had the resources or the inclination to take such a recommendation seriously. I knew what they were thinking: once my little holiday in Canada was over, it would be time to get back to work at home.

And maybe it was time that I pretended to myself I was on a holiday. All I wanted to do was go out on the balcony, have a cigarette, and take in the night sky. The pulsing lights of the cars threading through the tree-lined streets all the way up Mount Royal looked pretty from there. The view was almost beautiful enough to stop me from thinking about what I felt in my bones about this case. Everything was not going to turn out all right. It was too late for that now.

There was one thing Georg Barany had said, while he was luxuriating in the attention I was paying to his every word.

"What those who fake a painting don't realize is that every stroke, even the ones you paint over, are all still there in the work. There is not one gesture you can erase."

Back in the hotel, as I opened the screen door to the cool breeze, I thought of his words and hoped that Barany might have actually said something that was true.

25. Nataša Ružić: Notebook Two

Vancouver. I was expecting rain, dark skies, that damp chill in my bones like the worst months in London. I imagined the ocean was going to be forbidding. I pictured waves like dark marble, a gloomy, rocky shoreline. I have walked the Seawall through Stanley Park, with the warm sun on the back of my neck as I followed the paths through a forest. I love the smell of moss and rich earth here. The roses still in bloom, not dry and stripped of petals as they are in Toronto's August heat. It is all so lush and vivid in the soft summer light. The end of this stage of my journey was supposed to come down like a dark curtain, but as I sit here with my notebook, drinking expensive coffee on the front porch of a bed and breakfast in a quiet, leafy little neighbourhood, I feel a sense of peace—however fleeting it might be.

It is a feeling I haven't had since my time in England—the first place I felt something like true freedom and the possibility of forgetting. Despite how fleeting that too would become.

Once I arrived in England, what was clear to me within minutes of meeting my employers, was that the couple—David and Jennifer Benton—should not have been together, no matter how compatible they might have seemed at first sight. Both short and squidgy, as David himself called his wife, they looked like someone's grandmother had dressed them for church, she with a frilled collar and patent leather pumps, he in his Paddington Bear duffle coat and cable-knit sweater. But there was a simmering tension between them that boiled over into an argument over parking while we were waiting at the luggage carousel, and Paddington seemed to have no reservations about calling his little squidgy bear a cunt. We drove back to Croydon in silence. The back seat of their Volvo smelled faintly of vomit.

Over the course of the next five months, I learned much about their lives. Their marriage was a sad fiction, but I believe they sincerely loved Corin and Lucy—and with good reason. The children were indeed lovable, bright and full of life. I found myself becoming self-conscious because of how observant they were. Corin once told me I had a man inside me, one that came out when I spoke on the phone to Lila in Bosnian. He said it so quietly, as a question—"Do you know, Nataša . . ."—that it kind of scared me, as if Corin had seen my father's ghost take control of my voice. Lucy was much more reserved and unsure of me. She was independent and well behaved, the eldest girl already claiming her dominion. She was more slender and graceful than her brother and her parents. Her freckles were already fading and she looked to be turning into a beautiful, dark-eyed girl, who sang sweetly when she played the piano and did her maths homework diligently on the kitchen table. If my life in Croydon had been solely about Corin and Lucy, I swear I would have stayed on for the two years in the pathetic basement apartment next to the laundry room, saving what little I could scrape together for a fair start on my own in London.

But there was David to deal with. Three weeks into my job, when Jennifer was at a conference in Manchester with her boss, David came downstairs after I had put the children to bed. He said he wanted to tell me what a wonderful job I was doing. He had taken off his tie and undone one too many buttons on his shirt.

Without his jacket on, his belly looked like a little garlic bulb. He had a bottle of cheap sherry and two glasses in his hand, and a smile shone in his dead pig's eyes. He had tousled his blond hair in an attempt at boyishness but it looked rubbed in ashes. I could detect a drunken slur in his voice when he told me, with a raised eyebrow, as if I were in on the joke, that it was time for a little employee review.

The joke was on me. Once our drinks were poured, he stroked my hair, and had me sit on the bed with him as he told me how Jen-Jens wouldn't touch him since Corin was born. She wouldn't even care, he'd wager, if he and I had ourselves a little fun. "You know worromean?" I knew where things were going as soon as he came in, and when I remember it now I see it all as if I was hovering above my body, not feeling his hands tugging and tearing at my clothes, wrestling me down until he could get his little dick hard enough to shove it in me from behind. All the time he was cursing me, calling me his whore, while he moaned like a little boy as he bucked away. It didn't take long before he pulled out and I could feel his few drops of semen on the small of my back. As he slunk out of the room, he felt it necessary to inform me that Nick Priestley, Jen-Jen's MP boss, was actually his mate, and that if I decided to tell anyone about our new relationship he would make sure I was deported. I would never be eligible to leave "that little shithole where they breed you lot" ever again.

Through all of it, David had left the television on upstairs, probably to drown out any noise, and I remember there was some pop music magazine show on. That stupid song was blaring: "Maybe you're going to be the one that saves me, but after all, you're my wonderwall." No one was going to be the one that saved me, that was clear, no one but me.

As I write this I realize there is no way this can come out as anything but self-pitying and melodramatic, but here it is: it was around then that I had a kind of epiphany about suicide. I was in a Tesco, going from aisle to aisle, humming along to a muzak version of "Caribbean Queen." I can still see what was in that cart, all the crap from the frozen food section Jennifer sternly instructed me to purchase because Corin wouldn't eat anything else. But really it was her and David who seemed to subsist on no fresh vegetables at all, as if they had been weaned on pub food. The breaded chicken strips, the fish sticks, the frozen pizza from Germany were all stacked in their paper boxes, crowned with a sack of dried-out oranges from Spain, the only fruit I was ordered to get. As I surveyed it all I realized I was no different from a lot of the fake food there. I was a cheap export for the European market. My parents, growing up in those years under Tito, had at least been permitted to believe they could do work with some dignity, despite coming from villages that provided wealthy Europe with its janitors, house cleaners and construction workers now. My future was as fixed as cattle in the back of a truck. You saw their sad eyes through the slats of the stalls they were packed in; they knew what was coming. There in the aisle in my ridiculous pink tracksuit, my head full of tabloid thoughts and pop songs, I was as doomed, and the sole gesture of freedom I had left was to off myself.

Given what had happened to my mother and her conversion later in her life, I have an aversion to faith and believing in any higher being. But I will admit that in that aisle in Tesco, I addressed God in my head. That God fellow and I had long parted ways since Foča; looking back, I know I was desperate. There were tears flowing. Some chasm of self-pity had opened up and if I had been by myself in that basement flat I would have wept for hours. As it was, I dabbed at my eyes and tried for a look of concern, as if I were experiencing some allergic reaction. *If you really are there after being AWOL for so long, prove it, Mr. God. Give me some hope in my life again.* I wandered the aisles until the tears stopped flowing and headed back on the A212 to my little prison.

And yet, the craziest thing is, I still believe Mr. God answered me. As if he'd arrived late to the office, checked his messages and said, "Oh fuck, I better get that one sorted."

A few days later, bowing to pressure from Jennifer's mother, Corin and Lucy were sent off in Grandmommy's big green Range Rover out to Bath for the weekend. David suggested, as a token of appreciation for all my hard work, day after day (no mention of night after every few nights once Jen-Jens was off to bed) that I come with them into the city for the best bloody curry in Knightsbridge and then a little recreation at the Cloisters Casino, where David was on a first-name basis with the guys who presided over the blackjack tables. It was the first chance I had to wear the pathetic cocktail dress I had bought with the last of my savings in Sarajevo.

I will spare you the scene in the Indian restaurant where we sat next to a table of Jamaican-sounding drug dealers in pressed shell suits, and the argument over the bill that Jen-Jens insisted on having, and take you right to the moment in the casino where my life changed. With a wink and a promise not to tell his wife (I knew that wink well by then), David had given me two hundred quid to burn at blackjack. As I nudged my way into the front row to place my first bet, I saw Dragana. She breezed past on her way to the loo, dripping in gold jewellery, poured into her black silk dress, like a fucking goddess.

Well, what do you think I did? Of course, I barked out her name and ran to her, and we embraced like long-lost lovers. As I suppose, in the very back of my mind, I have always hoped we would have been. Corin, Lucy, David-and-Jen-Jens, the whole ordeal of living and toiling away like a slave for them, evaporated as she held me. I forgave her silence, her disappearance, her turning her back on home; I knew she had her reasons. *I mean, look at her!* She was with her date for the night, Sergei, who was upstairs playing Chemin de Fer for big money. I simply had to meet him but not now, no, let me get a pen, write down your number on a napkin, I'll give you mine . . . We parted with a can't-wait-to-see-you! in Bosnian, bellowed as she got into one of those old iron lifts where they stab people in French movies.

I used to think I was somehow ashamed about Dragana. I know how little I spoke to anyone about her, including Lucien. But now, as I write this, I realize there was another reason. So much about what we went through in London, starting from that moment, created a bond that feels sacred to me—at least the closest thing to sacred I've ever felt in my life. Maybe she and I weren't as happy and innocent as we had been at the Café Janus, but we became much more important to each other. I depended on her for my survival, and I know it was the same for her with me.

It was pretty clear what survival meant from how we met and how she looked. Of course there was no event management job, although Aslan, who got us both so much work, did indeed have a PR agency as one of his companies, and I suppose Dragana could have actually worked a few hours there at one time. She was dancing regularly in two clubs in Hackney, Ye Olde Axe and the Rainbow, but, just as it would be for me, the dates with guys like Sergei did not mean we were on the game. You could take the view that the clothes and the bling qualified as payment for services rendered; the truth is a little more complicated. There was protection and there were opportunities to make far more money than working in the clubs on offer every once in a while. And there was never any violence. We were always treated like ladies.

Weeks had passed since our meeting at that casino, and we were solely corresponding by email. She was upfront about her work, writing about the fact that Sergei, with his gold tooth and a dead eye from his time in Afghanistan, was more of a minder to her. He needed her for appearance's sake at places like the Cloisters. She wondered if he might have actually been gay. He could never have revealed that to anyone, given his role as a retired enforcer, even with the credibility he had from being ex-military.

Dragana emailed me about all the punters who'd come in and pay her for dances, in that way she had of making the unbearable hilarious. I would laugh aloud on the basement computer, so much so that David, in a concerned voice, asked me if I had been crying myself to sleep one morning (I think he was disappointed when I told him otherwise). In turn I wrote to her of my life with the Bentons. I tried to make it as funny as she made her stories, but I hardly succeeded. With comedy you're only as good as your characters, I guess.

Right away I began to plan for a time when she and I could be together, and it finally came with Grandmommy's birthday, and another weekend in Bath for the whole Benton family. I appealed to Jen-Jens rather than David, telling her that I had been reunited with the best friend I'd ever had, now working in PR in the city, how I was grateful for the trips I had taken with the family but --- perhaps she'd understand --- sometimes you have to have a girls' night out. Jen winked. "Of course, love, we'll be fine with the little monsters. You let your hair down for a weekend, we all need it once in a while."

I knew, even before I left that Saturday afternoon, that this trip into the city would change everything. I had scrounged every bloody pound note I could in preparation. All the savings I had amounted to just enough for a not-too-extravagant dinner, a cheap hotel, and return fare on the 109 bus from Brixton. But as soon I arrived at the Elephant and Castle station, Dragana laughed at me spending any money at all. Her perfume smelled a bit like marzipan, and now, all this time later, a hint of it reminds me of her, of freedom and the promise of money. In the taxis she told me she had taken double shifts all week to get the weekend off and that she had hit the jackpot on Thursday night with a leaf blower from Qatar who was pissed on cognac. Leaf blower, I discovered, was the term for a man who would come in and spray pound notes at a girl for hours. "You keep your money, you'll need it for your great escape." In our emails, we had never spoken of me escaping the Bentons, but she had read my thoughts, as she always could.

I still wonder about that night. Later, once we were both working, I discovered that the unwritten code of conduct included having your pager on at all times. You had to be ready, at a moment's notice, to get into a cab even on your nights off and show up looking flawless at a casino or in the back room of a club where, say, the lads from some football club had come in for a few bottles of Cristal, or where some producer friend making a gangster flick with Reza's money needed some company at the Groucho. If Dragana had indeed taken her pager that night, she was more than discreet. It simply never appeared. I can't help but think she and Sergei had discussed my London weekend, and how they might woo me to become one of his girls.

It was easier than they both imagined, I suppose. I was ashamed that the restaurant she chose for us was the first sushi bar I had ever been in, so I lied, said I could remember going many times as a child in Michigan (East Lansing, sushi capital of America!). It was a shame I couldn't quite remember how to use chopsticks, but it had really been a long time ago. What I did not lie about were the frequent nighttime visits of David Benton and his threats about my deportation if I had disclosed anything about them. She took it all in and nodded, then she took my hand in hers and told me I wouldn't have to worry about him or my work visa if I agreed to come join her in London, and work for Sergei and Aslan. I barely swallowed before I asked her when she would like me to move in.

I wanted to know how it had all started for her. Unlike me, she said, she had actually liked the work as an au pair. She had been living with a couple from Manchester, both estate agents, salt of the earth, and their daughter Victoria. There had been no drama with the Dinarica agency, either. She knew it was run by scam artists like Branko from the moment she walked into their offices in Sarajevo. But, like me, she had reached a point when it was not about leaving on one's own terms, it was about emigrating as soon as possible, whatever it took. "They won't give you trouble either, love. We'll make sure of it."

Her new career started when she was going out with Adam, a carpenter from Warsaw. He was big in all the right places but not too smart, she told me wryly. He had been her first—"and last, ha!"—boyfriend in London. Adam did some work for some Russians on some fixer-uppers, all under the table, and he took them up on their offer to remodel a couple of pubs into adult entertainment venues. It was Aslan-in-the-Astrakhan, as she called him—older, wiser, less flash than Sergei, with the face of a fat pasha—who spotted Dragana's talents when she met Adam at a pub one Friday night. Aslan openly recruited her, right there in the pub. Adam did not take it well, and challenged Aslan to a fight outside, which created a silence at the table he should have understood immediately. When she and Adam left the bar, he called her a whore for even considering Aslan's offer. Two weeks later, Dragana was doing her first shifts at Ye Olde Axe and Adam was nursing two broken legs from what was classified as an accident on the job, care of employees of the gentleman in the Astrakhan coat.

Dancing itself, she said, was the easiest part. She promised to turn me into a pro with a bit of lingerie shopping and a night in front of a bedroom mirror with a mix tape and a bottle of champers. It was theatre, she said, but with real money! And then she laughed, more out of delight that this meant we would be working together and, I suspect, because she was no longer alone.

As she spoke I saw that almost her entire her life was a performance, not only the dancing. In the taxi I had noticed she was dressed down in comparison to that night in the casino. No flashy print dress, no gold, no transparent stiletto heels. "When you're working, you have to be vulgar," she said. "You're a fantasy for very simple men." Though Dragana thought all men were simple, really. I thought of Lila, and how I would write to her that Dragana had indeed become the sophisticated actress we had always imagined. All I wanted to be was just like her.

Truthfully—and I say this with nothing but a little pride for work well done—I was better at this job. And I had more repeat customers. Maybe there was something a little too big, too TV-perfect about the way Dragana looked. And maybe she was a little too obvious about it all being just a performance. One month in, even with the percentage I had to provide to the house (that is, to Sergei), I was pulling in the kind of money an actress working on TV dramas back home would make—and it was the same script every day.

There was a brief incident, about a week into my stint at the Axe, when I got a call from David Benton, with the threat that he would be speaking to his mate Mr. Priestley about me abandoning my contract. Aslan sent two of his largest boys over to David's law office a day later, and that was indeed the last I heard about that sad little family. I still think of Corin and Lucy, and wonder how they're growing up. I hope whoever's taking care of them now has the guts to knee David Benton in the balls if he touches her.

Dragana and I moved into a new condo together in the right part of Brixton, and as the months passed I realized I was actually happy. The last thing on my mind was that there would be opportunities for career advancement, but then Dragana came home one night with a couple of contracts she said she wanted me to take a look at, and so began my brief career in the movies.

I'm sure the whole world knows about it. One thing about the Internet, if you look hard enough, it's all there, isn't it? Every moment we have ever been in front of a camera to make someone money, you can trust it is there. And, not too far in the future, probably every moment that's publicly and privately recorded will be on there somewhere. Although I performed under another name, I can only imagine what has been uncovered since my disappearance. Honestly, I don't know what these movies were called. And I have never gotten up the nerve, or drunk enough vodka and tonics, to sit through them. But I was told, by Dragana and by a couple of (male) friends, that I was "just okay" in the roles I played. I don't know if I should feel good about that or not.

It's a curious thing, I think, that what made me a good dancer was perhaps the same reason I was not so good in these movies. I could not embody a fantasy that well.

I've thought about this with Dragana, why she was more successful—so successful, in fact, that soon she left dancing altogether for the better money and the travel. I've studied the Polaroids I once took of us both, and I believe there is something about her face. With her almond eyes, her high cheekbones, it's almost Buddha-like. Do you know why the images of Buddha are so powerful? It's in the symmetry, the smooth contours, the blankness and ambiguity of the smile: you can project so much of your own imaginings.

Dragana had always wanted to go to Berlin. She had ambitions about being a theatre artist, the kind Milan would have had in his productions that toured Europe and around the world. She was always going to be adventurous, an actress on her own terms. You would be wrong in thinking that somehow, because she ended up making the sort of movies that she did, that the war back home had extinguished that ambition. I like to think that she became an even more radical artist, right to the end.

Sergei's associate, Maarten, who said he was South African, had hired us for a week's work in Kas, on the Turkish coast. There would be two videos shot at the summer home of some drug dealer from Bulgaria (Dragana found out—no one could ever keep anything from her). With a pool, its view of the coastline, and sleek interiors, you could imagine we were in LA or Miami or, more to the tastes of my clientele, some villa in the south of Spain. We had travel and all expenses paid, of course, but really, in contrast to the kind of money Dragana would make later on, we weren't paid that much. Sergei had spoken of it as more of a paid holiday than a foray into a whole new line of work. As soon as I had gotten off the plane in Antalya and felt the sun on the back of my neck and my arms, I really didn't care. I was out of filthy old London, and that was all that mattered.

Still, we were both nervous about the work. With the dancing, every part about the transaction was so codified, so much like theatre. We were by the pool the first night, looking over the scripts with Maarten and the two German guys we were to be performing with (honestly, I forget their names and so much about them except that they doused themselves with the same cheap lemony cologne), and I felt as if I were subconsciously willing myself to live through the kind of ordeals I had gone through in Foča. No matter how much we like to think we're at the mercy of fate, we do make choices. I kept looking over at Dragana as we read together, looking for signs that she might be thinking the same thing. After all, she had gone through it all too. When we had talked about it back in London one night, she said it had first happened to her before the war, when she was still a teenager and living in Split. She caught my eye and gave me a wink.

When our short read-through was over and Maarten rose to take the men back to the pension in town where they were staying, Dragana took me by the hand, led me to her room and produced what would get us through the week: a couple of grams of coke.

I had done a few lines before, but it had always been someone else's. I had imagined it was the same for Dragana. Drugs were a way of being social with Sergei and his friends, part of the rites of the private rooms in the clubs and casinos where we ended up on the nights we weren't working at the Axe or the Rainbow. And the rule was clear: nobody ever did drugs while working. A martini with a VIP was one thing, but blow could get the place closed down because you might be dancing for a cop. Dragana explained that she had gotten the bag off Maarten. It was the first time she'd ever bought some for herself.

I want to believe that she was telling me the truth then, but as I think back on what was to come in the months that followed, I know it was probably a lie. I sometimes think she had such a force of life in her because she was ruthlessly focused on flaming out on her terms: young, attractive, like all the stupid movie stars. But that would have required some higher sense of destiny and, if she and I were alike in any way, it was that we were both improvisers. We were making it up as we went along. She was better at keeping her own secrets.

True to those Buddha-like qualities I could discern in her features, she was capable of revealing deeper pools of wisdom to transcend the unbearable. A couple of nights into our little working holiday in that villa, she told me her strategy for performing, given how much it reminded us of how we'd been raped. "You know, these scenes we're filming, of course they feel violent. With men, they want to break something pure and strong, like they've been broken. But you stay pure and strong and unbreakable by resisting your own thoughts of doing violence. Then you take in the energy, think of how you can channel it to make you stronger." She was coked up when she said this, but she was lucid.

She was always lucid, no matter what.

How she described men: she could have been speaking of Dejan, I think. He picked the wrong woman to love, and maybe she would have been better off with him as well. Too late for such a rewriting of our fates.

Despite her talk of channelling her violent impulses, the problem was, as her addiction would make clear, it wasn't making her stronger. She was doing violence to herself. She didn't want more energy and life. That was cocaine bullshit talk. She needed the real little deaths, not of orgasms, which she told me she could only fake, but of drug-induced oblivion. Soon it would be the deadly pin-prick precision of the needle.

That was her chosen path to transcendence. But it is not mine. I have convinced myself I have a better way of transmuting all the dark stuff of my past into something pure, despite all evidence to the contrary with Dejan.

While I've written this I've had three cups of coffee, and it is now a cloudless afternoon. I should not be in the shade. I have plans and people to see in this city. I feel that I can be visible and as free as I used to be now—despite the wiser course of action I should follow. I have spent too much time in my head. Still, to get it all down feels like purging the worst of my past. And now, at least for today, it is done.

26. Luis Aquino

After all that rain, you'd think the lakefront here would have smelled better rather than worse. There was something metallic in the air, and it was different from when we were last down here, checking out the torched Mercedes Benz the morning after the blackout. Strange part of town. By the light of the moon, the lake looked like a garbage bag. I got a bad feeling as I drove along. A bat dipped and floated in front of the car before winging up into the poplars.

I got one old guy who saw some of it go down. He had been sleeping in a pup tent behind some ferns. He had a New Brunswick driver's licence; Denys Robichaud, age 46. Crane operator, fucked up his back on the job and got addicted to oxys and the bottle, he said. He'd been living out here for most of the summer and this was the first time he'd seen what he called a pleasure boat quite so big drop anchor close to shore. At a strange hour too—it must have been two, maybe three in the morning, he said. That's what got him up. I'm surprised he was actually sleeping. He looked like he had been awake for about a week.

He said he got a look at the name of the boat: *The Missus*. We ran a check on that immediately.

Denys Robichaud also said that only one person emerged from the boathouse where the homicides took place. It would have been no later than an hour after that boat anchored. It was a little guy, wiry looking, with what Robichaud remembers as dyed blonde hair. Anyway, Robichaud said this guy came out of the boathouse and walked out to the pier not once but three times with what looked to be big square frames wrapped in black. He couldn't tell what they were from where he was. He saw a bigger guy in a baggy, short-sleeved shirt with palm trees on it and a ball cap that he wore back to front come out of the cabin and take the cargo. The guy had long shaggy grey hair that caught the light. The dude handed the little guy an envelope before the *Missus* pulled out once again.

The bodies that we found in the boathouse were a sight, I'll tell you. They looked like they'd both been beaten with a hammer as well as knifed. If it was the little guy, he's got to be very dangerous. There were large, dark contusions in the front and back of the skull with the male, and, Jesus, with the female, rag-dolled and bloodied, it's like he almost took the back of her head off. Why even stick them both with a blade afterwards, that was my question.

It's got to be that guy who broke into Bollinger's place, I figure.

Vidler, Caroline. Thirty, Quebec driver's licence. Stepanović, Petar. Twenty-nine, also Quebec. Fortune called me and said they were both from Montreal and they've got a connection to Rebane. The woman had an art gallery or something. So great, it's exactly what that chick from Interpol was telling us. Once I got in the office and pulled up that file, I knew those were the names she had briefed us on.

None of us took her seriously. Yes, I'm as much of an asshole as everybody else here. The Chief is going to want the full story after this. Better come clean right now, I don't care what Fortune says about ragging the puck.

After whatever transaction took place with the *Missus*, Robichaud said he heard the anchor crank up and the boat taxi out. It looked like it was nosing stateside, he thought. I guarantee you that's where we'll find out that boat registered. Probably with an Indian, a cigarette smuggler. Those are the guys that have started working with the Russians and the cokeheads, they know the old routes and safe ports, the ones that haven't changed since the wops were running gin down to New York.

We had what we needed on Caroline Vidler's Range Rover. If that guy was stupid enough to still be out there on the road with it, maybe on the 401, we would have had him before lunch, that was for sure. But he wasn't, was he?

It all came together, in the worst way, when we found out the boathouse was owned by Alex Rebane. The property was in his name but by the look of it he hadn't had a boat in there for years. The Evinrude calendar on the wall was from 1988. So what had he been storing in there? Looked like nothing but some old paintings and furniture he once had at home.

So we could piece it all together, I figured. I told Fortune I had almost lost faith we'd find a lead. "But you gotta have faith, Aquino." That's what Fortune said. You don't want my faith, I told him. You look at what happened out here, you know evil is real.

27. Dejan Vidić

You have to understand I had come to the point where I could only look after myself. I sacrificed everything, okay? I had done bad things, but I swore to myself, after it all ended back home, that I would never go that far again. I did it for Nataša, and it was becoming clear she used me. That fucking Lucien of hers. Now there was no real money like she promised, and things had turned with Petar and Nikola. I was doomed. If I didn't do what I did, I knew Petar and him were planning to take us both out.

I could sense it in the weird silences on our final call. As expected, they would only agree to give Nataša a fraction of the money at the meeting with Nikola. When I suggested that might cause her to refuse and walk away, Petar laughed. "That's not the Nataša I know. But maybe you know something different, Dejan? Anything you want to tell us?" What could I say to that? My denial was only met with more dead air on the phone.

I was so nervous coming out of that call that I went to meet Petar again in that same hotel bar. He told me he couldn't leave Toronto even if they could finally get those fakes of Alex's to Mikha, who was coming up from the States. The cops had called him in once again, and now he was convinced they were going to find me.

"They'll do a much better job of finding you than you could

ever do finding Nataša, Dejan. But maybe she's already been found? Who knows?" He smiled. We were outside that bar as he smoked one of his rich girlfriend's cigarettes. He looked like a pimp in his all-white track suit and basketball shoes. "I'll tell you what I think you should do, buddy. I say we go dark on Nataša. Fuck it. Until you can find her, let's force her hand."

So I stupidly got upset, exposed my own impatience. I said he'd already talked to Mikha, so a deal was happening, money was going to change hands for the fakes. All he had to do was take control of the situation, send a transfer to Nikola and we could get this over with. He shook his head. "Can't. Couldn't do that to Caroline. What can I tell you? Guess I'm whipped. Can you imagine how that feels, buddy?"

After that meeting, that's when I contacted Mikha. I mean, I was the one who connected him and Petar originally through Aslan, back in London. So many ways Petar owed me. I got out of him what Petar agreed to after I said I was hoping to get him a couple more fakes. It was a lie, but one I knew he wouldn't call Petar about.

And then I headed over to the boathouse at the agreed-upon time and waited. Their car pulled up once it was dark. As soon as they got into that boathouse I made my move. I had a buck knife. I didn't expect it would escalate, but Petar came at me with a spade he picked up in that boathouse while that bitch made a run for their car. They gave me no choice.

You think I wanted to go that far? I puked afterwards, right there in the bushes. I could barely keep it together for Mikha. But I got my money. Not even four hundred.

Millionaires who could finally start a new life together? The whole idea would have made me laugh.

Once I got back to that motel I called Nikola on one of the payphones out front. I guess I must have looked like hell because a few people walking by, they were staring. I told Nikola it got out of control, I had no choice. It was all over as far as I was concerned. I practically ordered him to send the email to Nataša, I'd wire him the cash and then finally we'd get the tape and take Nataša out. What could he do but agree? I didn't care if he didn't believe me anymore.

The call with Nataša was next. Of course it went badly. I said look, if we didn't go through with getting rid of Nikola, we were both at risk. She was too far in to back out now. If she wanted to walk away from me and all our plans, that was fine, but we would split what money we had, I'd go my way and she could go hers. She was crying on the phone by the end of it, saying anything, anything.

And maybe I believed what I was saying. Maybe I hoped we could still try together. But I knew it wasn't going to happen, deep down. I knew I'd have to deal with her too. Not even four hundred thousand at the end. What a mess.

28. Milan Zujović

The stage was bare but for two wooden black boxes that some-body on the crew of *Lincoln in Twilight*, the last opera in this barn, had left behind. One of the boxes made a good bench where I could sit with my second espresso and think. I was trying to come up with a solution to the mess our third act had become. The crew were bringing in the new screens for the projections later in the morning—they'd been redone, the first versions weren't work-ing—but in the quiet of the early morning, I could be alone to concentrate, block out the world, read through all the scribbled notes I had made in my sleepless panic the night before.

This was two days before previews. I had a little more than ten precious hours in the space to make this cohere somehow. The problem, just as it had been in Chicago, was Cassandra. Her entrance and her long speech, where suddenly Golimov has so abruptly shifted the tone, come off like a scene from another work.

I did not hear the door open from the right wing into the orchestra pit. I was pacing out Cassandra's speech, intoning the words to myself, and I did not see Nataša emerge.

Standing there in the half-light, she called my name. It gave me goosebumps. Of course I swept her up in an embrace like a long-lost love.

"How did you get—? I didn't see you."

"The security guard let me in. I said I was your daughter."

"Thank God. I feared . . ."

She shook her head and pulled me close once more. "Nothing to fear. I'm fine. I made it."

"Look at you, you're a woman," I said, I couldn't help it. She seemed to retract, her smile tightening, her gaze shooting off away from mine. The only thing jarring about her was her hair, bleached white and pulled back in a tight little bun.

"It's been ten years? I better be."

"I'm so glad to see you. I mean, from what you told me, you know I was worried."

"Nothing to worry about. I've discovered I'm good at hiding from the world when I need to."

I motioned to a seat in the orchestra pit. She sat uneasily, poised to rise again in a moment, it seemed.

"You won't have to hide any longer. Listen, I've spoken to Mira. She understands. You can stay with us."

"No!" She raised her hand as if to shield herself, then tried to laugh to soften how forcefully she said it. "I mean, thank you, I appreciate that, Uncle Milan. It's just . . . Not yet."

"Not yet?"

"There is one meeting I have to take care of before that can happen."

"So you're talking to the police. Good."

She smiled and slowly blinked.

I told her my plan. "Listen, I have met the Consul General here. He invited Mira and me to a reception. If you've got a case, and you've got the evidence—"

"I have the evidence." She nodded and smiled with such steely calm. She looked so much like her mother.

"You know we'll do all we can. Let's get you to a safe place."

"I am in a safe place. Trust me. After this meeting, there will be no need for me to hide anymore."

"So come to the opening. Come see Mira, see what she's accomplished in the role. You still love the theatre?"

She gave me one of her old smiles. "More than ever, Uncle Milan."

"There will be a party afterwards. Right here in the theatre! Come and then we will all return to the place they've rented for Mira and me. It's big, too big for the two of us."

She finally seemed to relax, showing her pointy little teeth when she grinned. But she cocked her head on an angle, as if she were taking me in and didn't quite know what to think. Perhaps it was a question of trust.

"Thank you. Thank you, that would be nice."

"Good. Listen, I will leave you alone over the next two days. Do what you need to do with the police. There will be a ticket waiting for you, opening night, with an invitation to the after-party. How's that?"

"You take care of me. You've always taken care of me."

"It's nothing, you know. I'm glad, glad and relieved you're all right."

She rose from her seat and solemnly cupped my hand in both of hers. Then she kissed me on the cheek, whispered a thank you once more. Without another word she walked to the door that led out of the orchestra pit. She did not look back.

I could only stare up at the stage. I thought of a young actor Eva Vargas, my Cassandra for the last two productions. She would be here soon, earlier than everyone else so we could work on the scene. This whole process had been difficult for her. She'd lost about two kilograms, we had to alter her costume again. I had tried so hard to give her as much help as she needed, answering all the questions—so many questions—she asked each day to get her through the scene. This was our last chance to get it right.

And now at last I had something to tell her, as long as I could find the right words. All Eva had to do was move like Nataša, as if she was carrying the weight of some terrible secrets with her, into the house. I closed my eyes, rewound the fresh memory of Nataša once more. That look she had of a barely concealed grief. I had the little film clip in my mind now, and that was all I needed.

29. Christina Perretti

Caroline Vidler was dead. As soon as I heard I went to a coffee shop in Montreal and sat down. The oddest thing: I cried. This is a woman I was relishing interviewing after my meeting with Barany. I still had nothing but contempt for her. I don't think I fully thought through the trouble she was in. She made terrible choices, but she didn't deserve what had happened. It was all so awful. And for what? Fake paintings on a rich man's wall.

Of course now there was some progress in the case with Rebane. Detective Fortune told me that they found the artworks taken from the boathouse where Caroline and Petar met such a terrible end. Fakes Rebane had painted. They got them in New York. A Russian, Mikha Yakovlev, had placed them in a storage space in Buffalo. The man was not talking though; he was, as Fortune said, lawyering up.

We know Yakovlev has ties to Russian gangsters. That was easy enough to determine with his investments and his properties. But as for whom he got the paintings from, all he said was friend of a friend, before he called his lawyer.

The friend was no Russian. This had to be the man who had broken into Lucien Bollinger's house and assaulted him. They thought they had a lead now, though. They got into Petar Stepanović's emails and discovered a supposedly "very interesting message" sent by Nataša Ružić. There was a video clip attached, with old war footage from the former Yugoslavia. It was an attempt at extortion sent to Petar and two other men, Nikola Lazarević and a Dejan Vidić.

They found Lazarević. He was in Vancouver, working as a security guard. Though he was in custody, he too was not talking. Now they were working with the RCMP out there to bring Ružić and Vidić in. He was sure they had to be out there; it was now, as he said, a full-court press.

They had tracked Vidić down to London, working security in a place called the Axe. How appropriate, really. He had vanished. No one there knew where he had gone aside from on holiday. There was no record of anyone by that name either leaving the country or arriving in Canada.

His co-workers said he was an odd fellow. Kept to himself. Just once I would like to hear something different about such men.

This is really not my case anymore. I leave tomorrow. If there was a chance of recovering any forgeries Alex Rebane had painted or a chance of investigating the transactions of Caroline Vidler, that chance is gone, except our arraignment of Georg Barany. Anything that emerges from him, Rebane, and Yakovlev will probably take months.

Still, I can't stop thinking about Nataša Ružić. Fortune emailed me a blurry photograph which looked to be a still from a surveillance video. The time code in the upper left corner had been highlighted with bright green ink. The woman in the photograph was Ružić. She was unmistakable, despite having dyed her hair blond. The shot was taken from about a metre above her head behind a counter. The crown of another head was visible, a small cloud of grey curls—the person working at the ticket booth. Nataša was on the other side of a clear Plexiglas screen. The image was from a Greyhound bus terminal in Calgary, Alberta, and she was purchasing a ticket to Vancouver. She paid in cash. Fortune gloated about how they were sure to get her, sure to wrap things up.

Back in my hotel room, I ran the video clip of our interview with Bollinger. There were a few seconds of interest. It was at the point when I asked him how much he knew about her life in London. In the clip he says he was aware she lived through some terrible years—her parents murdered, many of her friends. He was aware she had worked in theatre and wanted to be an actress, but it was his impression that the war changed everything. She had gotten out of the country as a refugee, worked as a temp in London and met Petar by chance. They had known each other in Sarajevo, and he was the one who convinced her to come over to Canada and try it out. She had taken an interest in writing. He asked her a lot about that, given he was teaching her English initially. He said she was interested in how to tell stories. How they're put together. It was as if, he says, "she was in a process of transformation."

We had more, of course. We knew she had entered Britain with a working visa arranged by a firm that was being investigated for human trafficking. She was sponsored by a shell company traced back to a Russian businessman, Sergei Husev. Interpol has been watching him for years but hasn't got anything to stick. Yet. He has a typical profile of Russian mafia. Served in Afghanistan. When he returned, he fell in with small-time criminals. A car theft ring. He went to prison and came out ten years later as someone useful for some very rich men. Then he became rich himself from stock he owns in telecommunications, two natural gas firms in Kazakhstan, where he owns a home. A gangster who is inevitably going back to prison.

As for Ružić's tax files, she had been listed as an exotic dancer in three clubs we know Husev owns. From her passport, we know she travelled to Turkey two years ago for a holiday with another dancer. Husev has some business associates who were making porno videos there. I believe her relationship to him was probably defined as employee.

None of these things I could share with that poor, gullible Lucien Bollinger. But as I packed up and booked my flight I had a feeling he wasn't done with her. Things might still get worse.

I hate it when I turn out to be right about that.

30. Lucien Bollinger

I woke up the first morning I arrived here in Vancouver and glimpsed myself dimly reflected in the TV screen of my hotel room. Unshaven, with new bags under my eyes, I looked like I had aged a few years over just a few weeks. Sleeplessness and anxiety had turned me into the worst passport photo of myself. I rose, showered, and got dressed, took in the faded pink stain on the carpet, the smell of cheap bathroom soap. A vacuum cleaner was humming out a higher note of white noise with every lunge under an unmade bed next door. I realized it wasn't going to get any less gloomy as I drew the curtains on the grey blur of morning traffic in the rain. But this is where I had to be, waiting for days probably, hoping for the next call from Nataša. I had decided only I could save her.

The day after I had heard about Caroline and Petar, she finally called. I was walking home from the bus stop, my head down, taking in nothing but the sidewalk smeared with the first wet autumn leaves. I felt my phone buzz in my front pocket. A 604 area code. Vancouver.

"Lucien."

"Oh, thank God, it's you."

"Lucien, I had to call because I was worried about you."

"Where are you? Nataša, let me see you again. Please."

"Are you okay? I'm worried that you might not be safe. I know Dejan has found you."

"That man who broke into my place. Nataša, Caroline and Petar are dead. He did it, didn't he?"

"Lucien, can you go to the police? Get protection or something? He's capable of anything now, with anyone tied to me. I'm worried and I'm so sorry. I never imagined."

"Where are you? It's your safety I'm worried about, not mine."

"I am okay. I have to do this myself. I can't put anybody else in danger now. You'll hear from me soon."

"Do what? Nataša, let me get to you. You told me it's over, and that's okay now. I'll manage. I want nothing but for you to be safe."

There was a silence on the phone and then I heard the faint sound of her crying. "I'm not innocent, Lucien. It's best for you to forget me. I only want you to be safe. I only want you to know how sorry I am."

"I'm coming. I'm going to get to where you are."

"No! Please, Lucien. You'll understand soon. One way or the other. Please forget about me."

"Nataša . . ."

"And please go to the police and get protection. If you care for me at all, please . . . do it for me."

The line went dead. Within eighteen hours I was on my flight here. The only person I really wanted to protect was her. I was burning through my savings. But I had heard enough tenderness in her voice, enough of the promise of something like love, to know that I could not do anything else.

She was right about her concern for my safety though. A few hours after I had woken up in Vancouver I put my laptop and notebook in a backpack and headed out to the public library. I had not gone too far from the hotel when my phone vibrated in my pocket again. It was Timo, my building manager, asking where I was. My place had been broken into again.

"When you return?"

"I'll be back in a few days, Timo."

"Insurance, you need to call. You need to be back."

"I can't yet, but I'll handle it first thing when I'm there."

"You in some trouble?"

"Less trouble here than there." It seemed the best answer. I wasn't even sure if it was the truth or a lie now. "I'll let you know in a couple of days, Timo. Thank you for calling."

I hurried along through the streets until I found a coffee shop to collect my thoughts, assess what I might have lost. What did I care if Dejan had completely trashed my place again? Only my cameras and my photos were of real value to me. And it had been weeks since I had even thought about taking a picture. If I lost all my best work, would it really matter that much? With Nataša I was finally living in the present and not the past, finally thinking of a future that made me hopeful.

Coffee in hand, I found a table where someone had left a newspaper. I opened up the front section of the *Sun*, looking for the local stories, for anything to once again take me out of my own thoughts. I had to stop myself from trying, again, to see if anyone would pick up what was surely a payphone number that Nataša called me from. I almost scanned right past the story of the arrest of a local security guard. The picture showed an old, grey face. Lazarević, apparently a suspected war criminal, living in obscurity. An odd word to describe running from the past. Nataša . . . Was this what she meant by something she needed to do? *I'm not innocent, Lucien.* I scanned one paragraph after another for her name, but nothing. An ongoing related investigation, that's all the paper said.

I knew I was close. I wondered whether it might be worth going to the police to find out what they knew. But if Nataša was in hiding still, that proved they only had as much to go on as I did. Just enough to feel as useless as a stranger wandering around the city.

I continued through page after page of the paper like I was clicking through channels, looking for shiny flashes of images now, a little hint of beauty somewhere. In the arts section there was a photo of a woman dressed in a long white dress, wide-eyed, looking shell-shocked. The caption read Eva Vargas as Cassandra.

As I looked closer, the word Serbian pulled me in. Milan Zujović. I had heard that name before.

I laughed out loud. I rose from the chair and, even though it would be hours before the box office would be open for the first night, I knew exactly where I had to go. And where I would find her at last.

31. Nataša Ružić

I write this on the move to fill my sleepless hours. My third motel room in as many days. It is so much worse than I had ever imagined.

It is like I flicked a switch back on with Dejan, when he and I struggled with Alex in the sudden fear and confusion at his house the night of the blackout. I tried to keep things under control, I kept believing it might all still work—the money, the escape from our lives—but there is such violence inside Dejan. And now he has turned against me at last and will not rest until he has hunted me down. He wants me dead; he won't say it, but once he has what small amount of money I have left, what use will I be to him?

In our last call, we spoke about Nikola's arrest. With him now given up to the police, all the money from those fakes of Alex is now gone too. Out of our hands. In Dejan's shallow breathing on the phone, I could hear the desperation in his voice.

"I need your money. I don't expect anything more from you now. You whore. If you walk away from me without giving me what you have I will find you."

I tried to reason with him, tell him we should give ourselves up to the police. He would hear none of it. He said he had nothing to lose now and that if I turned myself in, I should be very careful. There are others involved now, others from my life he would eliminate.

I fear for Lucien, of course. I never should have called him, but I had to warn him. I fear he's going to try to be a hero for me. He has no idea who he is dealing with.

I even fear for Milan and Mira. I know that I mentioned Milan to Dejan, in all my foolishness, back in those days when we were briefly together in London. I had to boast of my education and my exposure to culture, I was so much better than what I had become. Now, with Dejan almost certainly here in Vancouver, I'm afraid he's watching them, and even if I reached out to them with a call or email, he'd be waiting for me to come out from hiding to meet them. But somehow I have to get to Milan.

All I can hope for is that no one in my world will suffer for my fatal mistake. I believed I could find some justice, find a way to make a new start in my life. I thought I could emerge a whole new being.

"Closure is an unhelpful term." So said Margit, the woman who took my rent cheques and lived upstairs in my place in Bethnal Green—my last home in London. Apart from Dragana she was my only friend in London. She had to be at least seventy, but was so well preserved, so well put together in her bright cardigans, her string of pearls. She told me she was a refugee herself. She had been a happy child in a small village in Hungary until the war began. A cloud of black years still darkened her memories. She and her brother were the only ones in her family who had made it out of Auschwitz. From the moment she first invited me upstairs for a cup of tea I was attracted to her. It was a kind of charisma she had: her command of silence more than her domination of the conversation was arresting. This kind of charisma is interesting to me, because I think it is the power created when a clean soul rubs away some of the dirt around the edges of your own, simply through the friction of real connection and conversation. "You realize you'll never be at peace with tragedy," she told me.

"And once I stopped believing it would ever happen, everything became easier."

There are two kinds of ways of being at peace, it seems to me. One is obvious—one's own death. Are we still haunted by injustice in the afterlife? I don't think so. The second is more arguable, but I believe in it more than I will ever believe in love or forgiveness: it is true justice. "What if you could get hold of the very people who decided you and your family would die? What if you could bring to justice the killers themselves?" I asked Margit. She told me she believed that the act of murder, even if it was carried out in the name of justice, irrevocably stained the soul, that it perpetuated an evil. To her, revenge was the source of all blood feuds, the source of the war she lived through.

Because there we were drinking tea and eating chocolate biscuits and calmly talking about what stained the soul, I told Margit about the rabbit. I'm still not sure why except that I felt that she, aside from Dragana, might be someone who would understand why it haunted me.

It is my most vivid memory from my first years, and it seems to mean more to me now than it ever has. We were camping, my mother, father and I, in Plitvice. I had gotten up early and wandered too far from the tent. My mother was too preoccupied with getting a fire going for coffee to pay attention to me. I remember walking behind a line of campers and cars in tall grass when suddenly a bunny's cute little head poked out of a coarse blue nylon bag, the kind used to store tools. The sack was grease-stained and torn. The bag moved as if the bunny was shivering, its one watery eye staring up at me as if to say, *little girl, come help me*. I thought to myself how nice it was of somebody to wrap the shivering bunny in the blanket. I approached to take him in my arms. But as I turned back the fold of the bag, I realized the nylon was smeared with gore and blood. The rabbit had been skinned alive, its heart visibly pounding. My mother said everyone in the campground was sure I had been attacked because of how loudly I screamed. She ran to me, gathered me up in her arms and carried me back to the tent, where she could safely slap and scold me not to stray from the tent again.

I know, from my own experience—I think of that rabbit skinned and still alive—that something inside me darkens and recoils from doing any violence to a living being. Of course I have felt the irreparable damage of the violence that has been done to me as well. The soul irrevocably stained.

I don't believe in any God, but if I were to imagine some great puppet master, I can't help but laugh at his bitter, dark sense of humour with Dragana and me. We loved theatre and dreamed we would be stars, and there we were, following our destiny all the way to Turkey, in a world we never would have imagined. You might say God even granted our wishes to be in front of the camera, to perform for who knows how many hundreds or even thousands of people. We were made immortal in the smallest sense of that word, our performances eternally preserved and available in the darkest corners of the Internet. How contemporary we were.

Now, with the camera I took from Alex's house, how strange it is that I cannot put myself in the frame. I can only record images with no people at all. I don't know what it means; I only compulsively record to shut my mind off. Maybe I should not question why.

Anyway, what I learned, during our time in Turkey, was that Dragana was more familiar with cocaine than what she wanted me to believe. She had presented the plastic bag as an incidental bit of indulgence, a way to distract ourselves from the nature of the performances we were being paid for in that house. She was tooting, as she called it, far too regularly, and with far greater resistance to the drug's effects than I could ever manage. Only a few weeks after we had gotten back she told me she was moving out of our shared apartment, that she needed a space of her own, and we both knew what was driving her away from anyone who could help her.

I think she was ashamed of the power the coke had over her. Worse, I believe she viewed me as someone who would judge her. She resented my insistence on working straight and putting aside as much money as I could. We argued more than once when she came home in the early hours of the morning and left the front door unlocked. At the time I tried to tell her it was not a question of me presuming I was somehow morally superior to her. My motives were far more self-interested: I was terrified that at any time I could be out of work. If that happened, I didn't want to be dependent on anyone else. I could have told her this but instead I became defensive and said that I had known she was addicted in Turkey, and that she was a bad actress and always had been. That did it. She told me she wouldn't care if she ever saw me again.

Over the next few months, from what I heard from Aslan, she had stopped dancing. Sergei said she was running with some dangerous characters, and that was saying something, coming from him. She had managed to find her own network of people in the porn industry, with her work in Turkey a calling card, I suppose. She had signed a few contracts and parted ways with everyone we knew, except Sergei's business associates.

I pushed him on it one late night, when we had gone out for a martini across the street from the Axe. I remember the Christmas decorations were in all the windows on that street. I was a little drunk and sentimental. It felt like the love of my life had disappeared. I wanted to know who she was mixing with, where she was living, anything Sergei could tell me.

"You really want to know?" I still remember how serious he was. He squinted and closed his fake eye. He knew it was distracting. "She's living in a tiny bedsit." He tapped his finger on his nose, indicating where all her money was going. "But dancing again. She's at Mirko's club. Out in Rotherhithe."

I did not have a clue who Mirko was, and Sergei was making it clear, fidgeting with his phone and his pager, that he really did not want to go into it with me. So I asked for an address and declared I'd find her myself. "Be careful," was all Sergei said when I left him to pay for my martini. "Maybe she shouldn't be found."

It is a strange impulse to be drawn back into the world of those who violated you, who were responsible for so much of your suffering. How can you explain it? Maybe it is because you feel directionless, without definition, without a new identity that feels authentic. There is something safe and reassuring about walking back into the cage. I saw it in Dragana. I felt the pull myself. Whoever Mirko was, I knew that whatever he asked Dragana to do, she undoubtedly would.

I made the journey on the tube to a place called The Swan near the Canada Dock. I had dressed as boyishly as possible, as if I were a student. I was prepared for anything, I told myself. There was nothing about Dragana's new life that would surprise me.

Nothing except the face I recognized working security in the club.

Back in Foča, after they had taken away the men, they detained all of us who were left—the mothers, daughters, the boys—in the Foča high school and the Partizan sports hall. I was in the high school, where I shared a mattress in the furnace room with two women, Jovanka and Melina Gudelj, a mother and daughter. I say their names to remember them, because no one else will. The mattress smelled faintly of ammonia. Faded brown stains ran across it like a map of dead lakes on a stretch of ancient desert. We were there for months, ultimately. The worst of our regular visitors were the men—many no older than students—who were in the JNA, or Yugoslav People's Army. They would often take both the youngest and the oldest girls and share them among two or three of them when they were drunk. The scar on my cheek was from the flick of a buck knife, a cut I received when I tried to defend Melina from them. She was thirteen years old. They raped us all many times.

When I entered Mirko's club I walked in past the bouncers who frisked the punters, and I felt a pair of eyes on me. Even when you don't look back . . . you can feel the dog look from men. That gaze of longing confused with something like revulsion. In this case it was even stronger. As soon as I looked up, glanced at his eyes, I knew it was a look of recognition. I had seen him before, the man with the white-blond hair. And though he had never touched me, we both knew he had done bad things, things neither of us could say we had forgotten.

Dejan. And what did I do? I said yes when he asked me out, like a moth that flies directly into a flame.

Dragana was indeed there and dancing, but she looked very different. She had lost a couple of kilos at least, and she had done her best, with her makeup, to conceal the dark rings around her eyes. Her breasts were so shrunken that her bikini top, all confetti glitter, really didn't fit her anymore. When she saw me, she shrieked from across a whole row of tables—in mid-lap dance—and gestured for me to hug her as if we were reuniting after some long journey. She had to be high.

At first, as we shared a drink at the bar, I felt the eyes of one of Mirko's lads on us both. He was periodically tapping his fake Rolex. I figured Dragana's state must be the result of her doing more heroin than coke, but, later, out in the cobblestone alley by the docks—an alley that seemed like it had seen a few murders over the centuries—she lit up a crack pipe and took a couple of hits.

I couldn't look. I walked back out into the streetscape built for the new money of that part of London, with its sodium lights, cameras mounted on the gates of driveways. Blinds down, ghostly words of graffiti scrubbed and turned to clouds on stone the colour of old dentures. I started thinking about how I would grow old. When Dragana came out, her eyes were like pilot lights. She looked crazed, and doomed.

But we kept up our patter. I tried to minimize the little interlude as best as I could.

"That bloke who works your door. The small one. What's his story?"

"Dejan? You mean Dejan? He's half-mad, him. He's a blast. Why? You think he fancies you?"

"I know him."

"You know him?"

"From back home."

Dragana got quiet as we marched in quick little steps, her heels like mallets striking the road, down to the corner to hail a cab. "They're all right, Nataša. Swear. Mirko thinks all of that was bollocks. Hated every fucking minute in uniform. People are people, he said to me. You remember that song?" She began to sing out, loudly, on the street. "So why should it be . . . You and I should get along so awfully."

And away we went, laughing. She and I, we got along despite the state she was in. I blame my own vulnerability, my own loneliness. I needed a friend who understood me unconditionally, and so did she. We had the past together, and that was my addiction.

Mirko had his own crew of old friends from back home, and, just as it had been with Aslan and Sergei, they had dominion over every aspect of Dragana's life. Everywhere we went together, even a restaurant around the corner from her wretched little bedsit, felt like we were fulfilling some role as accessories. There were nights in bad casinos out by the airport, long hours in pubs when Red

Star Belgrade or Partizan were playing, ringside seats for second-rate boxing matches, and clubs where the fights in the parking lots were more entertaining than who was on the card. I had a sense that Mirko might have been in a relationship with Dragana at one time, but it was clear, given her state, that he now took pity on her. The bouncers like Dejan were her last line of protection from life on the street, it seemed, so it was no wonder that she became for a brief period the girlfriend of one of the largest, dumbest ones, Nemanja, who went by the unfortunate name of Norman in his efforts to reinvent himself as an Englishman.

I dated a bartender named Alex, one of Nemanja's friends. He had a kind smile, and his brown eyes made me think there might be some spark of intelligence flickering under the manufactured dangerousness. We both knew our relationship wasn't going anywhere, and he could tell I was more focused on Dragana, as if I had become her minder.

It was in my relationship with Alex that I became more aware of Dejan in the periphery. We never spoke, but I always felt his eyes on me on the nights out with Mirko's crew. I could never figure out whether he considered me dangerous because of what I knew of his life back home, or if he fancied me. What I should have paid more attention to was that he never seemed to have a girlfriend. I remember asking Dragana what she thought about that, and she told me it wasn't that complicated. "I know his type. He only has eyes for you, sweetheart."

During the summer months, it was clear that Dragana was only getting worse. She said she was trying to stay off the pipe, trying to gain a little weight, but she was two months behind in her rent and not even able to attract the lowest punters with her dancing. Mirko suggested she wait tables for a while, but I had my suspicions, as did everyone who knew her, that she was on the game. She began missing her waitressing shifts and would not answer my calls for days. I couldn't walk away from her, though. I forced her to come out socially, despite how angry she became with me when I suggested she might need some help. I felt like I was the only one keeping her from complete self-destruction.

Soon after, Dejan and I finally became something like a couple. We danced around each other's past. And it was the strangest thing, in the silences, the reliance on gesture and touch; our intimacy created the closest thing to healing that I have ever felt. Even more than I could have hoped for with Lucien. I knew Dejan was broken like I was. But I suppose it was too raw, what he found in me. After less than a month I had to break it off, fully aware how much it hurt him.

And only I could find a way to make such a break even worse. It was during the hottest part of summer, those July days when London suddenly feels like a bad stretch of publand in Ibiza, when Petar Stepanović came over from Canada. He was close to Dejan and Mirko, but everyone knew of him and considered him somehow special—a success. I was introduced to him at the bar in Claridge's with Mirko, and he seemed like a pop star or a football player. His perfect tan, his lean torso in his rumpled linen shirt, how casually elegant he seemed. The champagne probably helped. As he and Mirko chatted, I butted right in and asked him what he did, he seemed so confident and well off.

"Well off? Hah. I wish I was. Maybe if someone buys my art, I'll finally make some money."

"You're an artist?"

He smiled and gave Mirko a wink. "I try. And you, you're an artist too, yeah? I can see it in you."

I really can't remember what I stuttered. It didn't matter. He could tell what was happening.

Infatuation really is such a ridiculous process. Your own hopes and aspirations for your life flood in when you encounter

someone who embodies an ideal. They drown out your better
thoughts, your sense of caution and realism. I had never met anyone who could call themselves a successful artist—and Petar just
had to be, despite his performance of humility. I mean, we were at
Claridge's, and he was staying in a room that would have cost my
month's rent for one night. Of course I looked at his hands—no
ring! How had this prince appeared among the pack of criminals
we had fallen in with? In my desperate frame of mind I decided I
was meant to meet Petar. Finally, here was a man who could provide me with an escape, and help me heal.

He had come to London to take in some gallery shows, he said.
He was doing a little talent scouting for his own space, which he
ran with his partner, whom he only referred to as a smart busi-
nesswoman. To my mind, nobody referred to their lover like that;
he was still available.

Yet more than the scouting, he said, he was doing some research for his video installation, and there was a mate of Mirko's,
a guy named Franjo who had some old footage of the war back
home he hoped he could look at.

Petar and Mirko began speaking of people they knew, and he
only seemed more special in my eyes. Here he was, a successful
artist, someone legitimate in the eyes of the world we all wanted
to live in, yet he hadn't forgotten all his old friends. When Mirko
told Petar that some months before that he had run into Dejan and
offered him a job, Petar was both surprised and delighted. "Dejan!
This is my oldest friend! He was such a fighter on the pitch."

I honestly thought I had made no impression at all on Petar, yet
as I was getting into a cab after the third or fourth club we had all
gone to, he pressed the business card of his gallery into my hand.
"You should call me tomorrow. We're supposed to see each other."

It was his "supposed to" that really got me thinking. When
you are as desperate and insecure as I had become, anyone who

tells you they have some intuition about your destiny becomes important to you. Petar knew how to exert that power, too, by how offhand he made it seem. The next day I went out and bought a summer dress that revealed my pale little shoulders, and new heels that made me almost feel sexy. If it was meant to be, I was going to be ready.

He took me for a glass of wine first, at an Italian place near Covent Garden. He had heard they cellared some great Barolos, he said, and wanted me to taste what a real one was like. He ordered a scotch first. He needed it, he said, after his trip out to Croydon.

I asked him about Franjo, and he fidgeted at the knot of a thin red cord around his wrist—one like the pop stars wore in the weeklies—as he told me what his visit was about. Franjo was practically a recluse here in London. He had worked for a while as a video editor at the BBC but now did freelance work from his small, cluttered apartment. Petar had known him back home, when Franjo was a bit of a maths prodigy and had become a national chess champion at sixteen. Petar could still picture that chubby kid in class, with a big cloud of hair that became a shapeless afro in high school. All these years later, at least he had found a barber, but he couldn't even maintain eye contact when he talked to you. "The war fucked him up. Like the rest of us."

What Franjo was reputed to have, owing to the fact that a German videographer had an apartment in the same building as him in Sarajevo, was a cache of old footage of some of the early days of the war. The videographer died when their apartment block was shelled, and Franjo, picking through the rubble, took what hadn't been destroyed. It was Petar's idea that he would create a video installation that mixed clips of his time in the army with footage he would tape himself on a trip in the fall. He was happy to purchase the old footage—money was not an object—but he needed to know what Franjo had. Franjo had not responded to Petar's requests by email, though. It was as if their old acquaintance meant nothing. So he had to go out there to Croydon himself. Mirko had his address, so Petar rented a car, drove out and found the little row house.

I asked him if he had gotten what he wanted, and Petar nodded, running his hand across his chin as if to straighten out his crooked smile.

He said they had watched old footage for a couple of hours. Franjo would hardly look at the screen though. He had watched it all dozens of times. He knew where Petar had some screen time, as they say in the porn business. He mostly looked out the window and chain-smoked. Once Petar had realized how much footage of himself was there, he took out his chequebook and asked Franjo to name his price. "Take it all," Franjo said. "Get it out of my house." He was completely resigned and disinterested, as if he had expected Petar or somebody else who was videotaped at the time to show up and, like a raid from the secret police, to confiscate what he had.

Petar took his last swallow of scotch and looked deeply into my eyes. "I think Franjo has psychological problems, you know? He's never recovered." I nodded. I knew exactly what he meant, of course.

The video installation project Petar was planning was a deeply personal thing, he said. He wanted to make it an exorcism of the demons of his past. Now, after his visit, he also wanted to dedicate it to Franjo as much as his late father, an art teacher, the original inspiration for the project.

We slept together that night, in his hotel room. And then the next night, and then the next. By the morning of his departure, I had resolved to find a way for us to be together. If he couldn't come to London, I would go to Montreal, it was that simple. We were meant to be.

There were so many things that I did not ask Petar about, stupidly—the real terms of his relationship with his business partner, how he made so much money, his friendship with Dejan, and what the demons of his past were and what was on that videotape—and this despite me knowing he was an old friend of Dejan's.

I know what my old Hungarian landlady would have said about how incurious I was. "Some people think denial is a river in Egypt," she would have said, and cackled to herself.

Petar and I emailed each other for a couple of months before I made my intentions clear. I played it as coolly as I could at first, telling him, in the drollest way I could manage, about my work and all the absurdity involved in performing the way I did, day in, day out. I admitted I had even let a few geezers touch me to see if I could force a stroke or heart attack out of one of them. I could tell this kind of talk actually turned him on, just by the flirtatious tone we both eased into. My sense was that if he was at all involved with that Caroline woman, he was hardly happy in their relationship. I waited for the right moment to question him about that, and then I told him he needed me over there. He never answered my question but he agreed that he needed me.

The next four months were my happiest in London, despite what I was watching happen to Dragana. Petar had promised me he could get me work for six months in his gallery in Montreal, and longer if it all worked out. As far as I was concerned there was no question of that. He would fall in love with me, Caroline would be out of the picture, and he and I would live happily ever after. I had a plan, a reason to get up each morning. I had an escape.

I was still trying my best to be the dutiful best friend, calling Dragana every couple of days, booking us in to go to the Vietnamese mani-pedi together, but she was becoming more and more unresponsive and erratic. She had moved a few streets over to a smaller and even more squalid place, where her underwear hung to dry on the shower-curtain pole and her tiny closet looked like it was exploding with hooker clothes. Her relationship with Nemanja had ended long ago, and she made an impulsive decision to try to fall in love on the rebound. She told me her last guy had to be sixty, a mad old fucker who had told her his father was an earl, still alive, and he had been cut off financially after doing time on a heroin trafficking charge. She said she foolishly supported this waster for a while, and it was clear to me the money she made was no longer from waiting on tables. I felt helpless to pull her out of her tailspin, and I had indulged myself with my own romantic fantasy about Petar to the point where I felt I didn't have the energy. The spotlight was on me, not her, for once.

I think about those last few weeks before I had left for Canada and wonder how things might have been different now. Maybe Dragana and I should have had a huge argument, where I screamed out my pain at seeing what she was doing to herself. She would have screamed right back and sworn to cut me out of her life. But I know it would have only been a few days later that we would have been reconciled. Would I have been able to help her finally get clean? Some days, when I hate myself a little less than usual, I feel that there was nothing I could have done. But most days I feel like I didn't do enough, and that I abandoned her at the one time in her life when she needed a friend—when she needed me—the most.

There was no talking me out of leaving, even though one particular person tried. I had told only a few people that I was making plans to go, so it was a surprise to me that, about a week before, during one of my last shifts at the Axe, Dejan came in, ordered a double shot of cheap Polish vodka and took a table directly in front of the stage. I could tell by the redness in his cheeks and his ears that he was drunk. He rocked in his chair as if he were on a boat, and he would not return my smiles in his direction. I went over to him to say hello. He took my arm, said we had to go and talk. The muscle at the door that night was a local, Morris the Minor we called him, and he knew Dejan well. Bouncers—it is like they have their own trade union. Morris gave him a look of warning, but Dejan waved him off, mumbling that there was nothing to worry about. That was all it took: nobody who knew Dejan fancied the idea of telling him how to behave when he was drunk. He led me into the cloakroom, despite my protests. In there the music playing from the stage was not quite as loud. The wool coats smelled of rain. Once the door was shut he poured out his heart—his phrase. I couldn't leave, didn't I realize that he still cared for me . . . When he heard about Petar and me, he couldn't take it anymore. He had been drinking heavily every night since then. He told me that Petar was deceiving me, he was a con man, and that from the moment he saw me, all the memories of that horrible time came to him and that he knew we were destined to meet again. I would be his salvation, and he would be mine if I let him. And then he started crying, pleading with me not to go. How could I be so blind, he said, not to see how much he loved me?

My cruelty, my foolishness: I insisted, as gently as possible, that I had to see things through with Petar, I had to get on a plane. Dejan took it with a soldierly nod. He murmured that he would always love me. *I don't think you know what love is*, I thought. *I am really not sure what it is either.* But I was wise enough to stop myself from saying those words. I simply reached into a few coats, stole the first pen and scrap of paper I could find and told him to write down his email address, I would keep in touch. "I must do this," I said, "I can't explain well, but maybe I will find the words and send them to you."

Fulfilling that commitment was my fatal mistake.

32. Georg Barany

There are so few genuine painters. My father Ferenc was one. I could show you paintings of his and, if you knew anything, you would say his talent was the equal of some of the greatest painters of the twentieth century. But he was born at the wrong time. If the Russians had seen some of his best work, he would have died in the gulag. He was cunning enough to survive. And to escape. For the last thirty years of his life, he painted every day while he worked washing dishes, driving a taxi, doing anything to keep my mother and me with a roof over our heads. He died poor, alcoholic, and broken. He couldn't choose the age he lived through; he could only choose each brush stroke on a canvas. And art is never enough. There are so few genuine painters, and now my father has his own page in their story, what I would call the secret, real history of art in these times.

Alex Rebane is in that book now too. You could say he was blessed with good fortune, and not once but twice. But what I liked about him was he couldn't give a damn. He was ruthlessly mercenary. You know Rimbaud? If you do, you know he died a gun-runner. Well Alex, he was just like him. I'll never be ashamed of our working relationship. He made better fakes than ninety-five percent of the original work that hangs in the homes of millionaires in this country.

And I'll never be ashamed of my trade. If I injected a little de-stabilizing toxin into the bloodstream of a market already dying of its own cancer, well, what is the harm? If anything, now the corpse is laid bare and you can judge for yourself how much of the viscera are blackened with bad money.

I first became aware of Alex through a movie producer, Toby Levin. He was a client of mine who, in the years when he had too much money, opened up his own gallery in Toronto. One afternoon he took me out for a six-hour lunch in Yorkville, plying me with glass after glass of Barsac until he presumed I was drunk enough for a private viewing in the top floor of the gallery space. He wanted to test my eye. Because Toby Levin was a great lover of fakes. So there we were, taking in his two Riopelles, his Morrisseaus (he needed to be seen as a great patron of Canadian work) and one "stunning" (his word) Harold Town. Except the Town was not a Town at all: it was Alex's work.

Toby had gotten to know Alex when a movie he was working on needed a couple of fake de Koonings for the footage they were shooting in Toronto. A woman in set design who knew that Rebane had returned to Toronto, and was almost broke, suggested he might be able to paint them—as long as his name was left out of the credits. That was the start, Toby said, of a beautiful relationship. "You see that Town? Between you and me, I'm one glass of wine away from taking it downstairs and selling it as the real thing."

Toby eventually did, among a few of Alex's fakes. He's a master showman, he deserves his Order of Canada.

It couldn't have been more than a month or so later, if memory serves, that Caroline Vidler came to me. She wanted to authenticate a Soutine she had gotten from a friend in Holland. That creep Stepanović was accompanying her, so I really didn't have to ask about her friend; I figured it was stolen. I liked Caroline.

You know her grandfather was Constant Vidler? He ran an auction house in London that became embroiled in a scandal about fake antiquities sold to some very well-placed friends, including two ministers in the Attlee government. Caroline had come to embrace the family trade and was nothing but charming about it.

I asked her if she had a buyer for it already. I was thinking of a few clients I had helped out who would have no compunction about purchasing, even if the provenance might be dubious. She had one in Toronto, she said, someone she had sold a Harold Town to, and that triggered my thought that one might be able to sell the Soutine to two people—if you knew the right person who could create a flawless fake. It would not be in anyone's interest, after the sale, to make their purchase known, given it was no doubt stolen to begin with. And so a prosperous revenue stream was created for both of us.

Or should I say all three of us? Alex Rebane did very well by the work we gave him.

It was Stepanović who ruined it. He had connections to Russians who wanted good fakes, as well as stolen paintings from Europe that could be forged and sold on the black market to more than one customer. Petar positioned himself as able to provide an endless supply. Some of the work had originally been stolen from families during the war, so no one remained to refute questions of origins anyway. Caroline should have realized what she was in for.

Now I know this probably couldn't have ended any other way. But if you think I'm going to spend my last years in prison, think again. I have an expensive lawyer, and information everyone in law enforcement will find valuable. I learned from my father many years ago that all things are transactional. Better put all your chips on the table.

I'm ready to do that. And I'm ready to cash in.

33. Alex Rebane

Dear M.,

I have been reading about what is believed to be your last work, the Martyrdom of Saint Ursula. I looked at the plate of the painting in a new book I have, and there she stands, an arrow stuck in her chest, her murderer, the king of the Huns, standing right beside her. The story is that the king captured her, along with eleven thousand virgins. The king's men killed them all, but he was so enraptured by her beauty that he let her live and asked her to marry him. When she refused, he shot the arrow that pierced her heart. It is a stark, cruel little scene—it would have made a good final painting with Nataša.

And there you are among the men observing the murder, with your gaze uplifted, your tired eyes and pale, drawn features catching the light. You were suffering from an attack on your life in Sicily. Perhaps you're imagining your own death. I'm sure you always thought it would be violent.

I try to imagine my own last work and what I would want it to be. I have never painted myself. Maybe it is time I began to try.

I regret I didn't when I was younger. It would have been of value to me to compare how I would have painted myself at twenty-four, when my work first began to attract attention, and the portrait I would want to attempt now.

There would be no martyrdom in the scene, I can tell you that. I would only put myself in the foreground, like old Rembrandt, and I would gaze at you head on, with all the defiance I have left. It would be a defiance not of death but of final judgment.

Yes, I would not even accept your judgment on the figure I could manage to paint now. You, the only one whom I would trust to see me clearly, with true depth of field.

I am tired. I have been up all night and here comes the morning. I'm feeling morbid and sentimental about myself, and I know, in this state, that this is not the time for me to write you. I can tell you loathed sentimentality.

But is it not good to imagine what your final work would be? There is nothing like a hanging, as Mr. Johnson said, to focus the mind. I have escaped a few nooses, but I'm not the young Houdini I once was. Nor would I want to be anymore.

I'm sure, all you would want to tell me is to make the last one real. That is all you could claim in the end.

Words to take to heart—like an arrow. And to sleep on, at last.

A.

34. Nataša Ružić

Just hours before Milan's opening night now. There is nothing more I can do.

I'm escaping myself as much as Dejan, though I've given up on escaping judgment for what I've done. What a foolish notion to begin with—to think that it would have ever been possible.

My life in Montreal was worse than I could have imagined. When I got there, once I was settled in a room in a house full of university students, I discovered that my work as a gallery assistant for Petar and Caroline required me to be little more than a slave for that bitch, picking up her dry cleaning, taking her cat to the veterinarian, making sure she had her cappuccino prepared just so from the café around the corner at eight-forty sharp each day. No matter how Petar tried to minimize it, it was also obvious they were still in a relationship. He had told her that I was an old girlfriend of his who needed to get out of London, that he was doing me a favour.

My feelings for Petar were rapidly changing. I had begun to realize, above any claim he could make to being a creative artist, that what he truly possessed were great powers of improvisation. He could come up with plausible motives in the moment and explain them so eloquently that it seemed like even he believed them. His best performance was back in London soon after we had slept together, when he rhapsodized about how he felt more "intuitively connected" to me because it was as if I emerged "from the true Sarajevo we both remember." I "carried his home" in my heart, in my every word and gesture. I think he realized what a fantasy this was, how I was never more than a fuck on the side, when he saw me rebel at my submissiveness to Caroline and recoil from the shame he felt at how she dominated him as well. Just from watching them both in the gallery, I could see that he was a kept man. Caroline was the one who controlled the finances, who promoted him as an artist, and he, from what I could see, did little more with his days than shop and prepare their dinners, and talk on the phone to all their phony friends, these parasites who called themselves curators and tastemakers and lived on trust funds and their cut of the shit work they sold to the local new money or, if they were lucky, to Caroline's network of Russian, Chinese, and Israeli millionaires. His so-called video installation was a mystery project. He never spoke about it again, and I was convinced he had walked away from it. When I had arrived I wondered what he could possibly be doing with a woman like Caroline Vidler, and after six months, despite how horrible she was, I was now wondering what a woman like her could possibly have seen in him.

That December, things finally came to a head. I had gone down to Las Vegas to help Caroline during an art fair that she gushed about, saying it would rival Miami, Art Basel, and Frieze. There would be at least three hundred UHNWIs (ultra high net worth individuals, as Caroline explained to me with a sigh of exasperation) for three days at the MGM Mirage. I was supposed to feel grateful for the opportunity to trail behind her in that theme park, collecting the cards and taking in the toxic cologne fumes of all the Russian gangsters she met. I fetched her breakfast, plying her with these awful nutrition bars anorexics eat, and made sure the kind of gin they served her was her favourite English brand.

Petar was back in Montreal sulking because he had yet to create anything that anyone was interested in buying, which only gave her more licence to treat me like the help. I was about to quit and find my own flight back to Montreal on my maxed-out credit card when she allowed me to join her to meet Alex Rebane over cocktails at the Dolphin bar. She loved him like a brother, she told me. Two drinks in, I knew I had found someone with whom I could forge an alliance until I sought my independence.

In all my time with Caroline, our attraction to the same men was the only thing we had in common. But my relationship with Alex was very different. It was based on me consenting to be his subject.

Our moment of connection happened while he and Caroline got into an argument about Petar. I realized, as she was going into great detail about Petar's faults, it was no sudden whim of kindness why I was sitting with her and Alex. That I had slept with Petar angered her, humiliated her, and now she was going to make it clear to me she had the power to dispose of him. It was impossible for Caroline and me to talk as equals, impossible for her to ever admit she was hurt by Petar's betrayal, because of course she knew his story of me being an old girlfriend from back home was a lie. No, she had to diminish him to the status of an accessory, exactly as she had been doing with me since I had arrived. Alex, bless him, would not play along. He chided her, saying Petar gave her some grit in her life. She was an abrasive, entitled princess without a boy who gave her trouble. All men were boys for Alex, even when they were men in their sixties who bought his art, it seemed. To irritate her, he started asking me questions about myself, and he quickly intuited what was really going on once I told him I was a friend of Petar's. The more I spoke, the more I became some object of fascination for him.

"I want to paint you wearing a gold ring on every finger, but with dirty fingernails," he said, as he took my hand in his. His gaze was childlike, like a boy playing with a doll that had come to life.

I laughed, told him he knew me too well. I still really don't know what I meant by that.

"I'm serious! Can I paint you? Would you come to Toronto for a weekend and sit for me?"

I still hate that I looked to Caroline at that moment, as if I needed her permission. She looked away, nervously tinkled the ice cubes in her gin and tonic. "I would love that," I said. Caroline rose from the table, muttering that she needed a cigarette.

That first weekend in Toronto, over the hours I spent in Alex's studio, he felt comfortable enough to talk about himself. A lot. It wasn't as if he was completely incurious, it was that he had his own version of me that was more important to him. He wanted to portray me "like a Freud." When I told him I had never read any psychology he showed me a big coffee-table book of Lucian Freud's work. As he worked away I asked him how he had gotten to know Caroline and Petar, what else he was working on, who he was seeing. Alex had built his life around so many secrets that speaking to me was like a release valve.

In the course of our conversations I had to ask about his opinion of Petar. Did he think he was an artist as well? Had he ever seen his work? He laughed, said Petar thought he was. He had been encouraged by a coterie of academics while he was dodging welfare as an art student in Montreal to believe that he had some talent. At first he had called himself a performance artist and then gradually he came to believe he could paint and make videos. He spent a couple of evenings showing Alex all his work. Now, whenever they met up, Petar insisted on talking to him as—Petar's term—a fellow artist. His understanding of Petar's and Caroline's relationship was that she had gotten involved with him for mercenary reasons, and now she had to live with the fact this fool actually thought he had a career.

I returned to Montreal determined to escape my circumstances. If I had to dance again or worse, I didn't care. Only my visa was keeping me with the gallery. I had managed to get out of my obligations once before in London, and I would do so again. Caroline could sense how I was feeling and spoke to me with a new detachment that emboldened me. Petar had retreated into his own house-husband's duties, it seemed, rarely coming to the gallery. I am sure he viewed me as a failed project; he was waiting for me to do something about it.

Soon after that trip to Toronto I received an email from Dejan Vidić. When I saw his name in my inbox, I suspected it might be some declaration of love. But no, for once he was unpredictable. It was a terse message to tell me that Dragana had died the previous night. She had hanged herself in her washroom. He thought I would want to know.

I wept for what seemed hours on the gallery floor. Finally, I pulled myself up, and smoked what must have been my twentieth cigarette as I wrote Dejan back and thanked him for thinking enough of me to let me know. And then I walked out of the gallery, fighting back tears, explaining to Caroline I had a personal issue. She would have been happy to fire me in that moment, and probably the only reason she didn't question me was that she didn't want it to get back to Alex that she was so horrible. I had found myself a powerful ally despite myself.

I started walking and ended up at the Notre-Dame Basilica. You know I don't give a damn about any religion, and I certainly did not want to suddenly convert, to offer myself up to some higher power. It was merely about the sense of quiet and peace in there. I loved the azure ceiling, the golden stars. I remembered being homesick for Sarajevo in my first few months in London and looking up at the sky one night, when I had gone to smoke a cigarette on the roof of the Axe. The same sky over my head that arched over the channel, over the towns and cities lit up like the motherboard of some junked computer, full of the old corrupted files that made up Europe, reached all the way to that city that had once been my home. I felt some sense of consolation then. Now here I was in another part of the world, and the sky was a painting. There was no consolation, I was truly alone in the world now, and yet I knew I didn't want the real sky anymore. All I had was the painted blue, the painted stars.

Over the next few days, back at work, I noticed that all the videotapes that Petar had purchased from Franjo were on the second floor of the gallery. They were stacked on a drafting table in a part of the room that was called Petar's workspace, perhaps in the hope that he would actually do work there one day. I didn't touch them. I knew their potency.

It was only when Petar came to Toronto, when I was modelling for Alex, that I had the courage to look in on what went on as he worked on his so-called project in Alex's annex. That was when I came upon Alex's fakes too. So many revelations . . . It all turned so fast.

I brought the first few up to Alex's room when he was out of the house because I knew he had a TV and VCR up there. I remember my hands shaking as I held them. The videos had been made during the years of my innocence, when Dragana and I were still so full of hope and ready to take on the world. The videographer had labelled where they were shot too, so I figured there would be images of the streets where I grew up before the shelling. Four tapes near the bottom were labelled *Foča*, with the dates corresponding to when I was there.

I remember Lucien asking me, on what was our third date, if there was one movie that had changed my life. We were in a line-up outside a rep cinema to see the Tarkovsky film about a painter. I think Lucien believed that would be something I would like. I didn't. I had seen it as a kid on TV and thought it was boring, something my parents would force down my throat. I honestly can't remember what I told Lucien in response, but it doesn't matter. The only answer that would have been the truth was this: a video called *Foča 07/12/92*.

It is not a great piece of filmmaking by any standard. It is raw footage, unedited. The camera jerks this way and that in the streets of the village and later, about six minutes in, in the outlying countryside. The audio is terrible throughout, but it doesn't really matter, there is no dialogue. It is the work of one man frantically recording the day troops from the BSA came in and rounded up men, as they had been doing for a few months by that point, and took them out in the countryside and murdered them.

Only one scene matters to me. At the eight-minute mark, there is my father. It is the last recorded image of him. He is being marched along the road to a clearing in the forest. There were two soldiers I recognized immediately. One was Petar and the other was Dejan. Tell me it was not fate we would come together again. The camera does not record the executions. There is the faint sound of the shots. The videographer was recording from the safest distance possible, that seems clear. The sound of a truck's engine, somewhere along the road and getting closer, and then the screen goes black. The whole segment is not even a minute long.

When I returned them I came upon Alex's fakes. They were there at the back of the annex, a couple of paintings that bore no resemblance to anything he had created in the studio. They were in the style of old Soviet constructivists; I knew that work from my school days around the time of the breakup of my country.

It couldn't have been more than a day later that I asked him about them when we were working in the studio. At first he was angry, telling me I should not have been snooping around in what was none of my business. I got angry in turn, calling him a fraud. He laughed, said I was a child, that I had a lot to learn about the world.

"What are you going to do with them? Is it a prank?"

"Darling, it's more than a prank. They'll probably net two million dollars."

After our conversation, I did my best to hide my disgust and disillusionment. For days afterwards I felt depressed. I couldn't see Lucien, couldn't talk to anyone. I could only write, but even my words felt fake, and I ripped them up. I had admired Alex so much, but he was no different than Petar, a criminal.

The implications of the Foča tape had begun to dawn on me though. Not only could it destroy Petar's career, it could blow a hole in Caroline Vidler's life, and that could lead to wider revelations about how she ran her side business. Inevitably Alex would be discovered too.

I wanted to escape from them all. It dawned on me that, with the kind of money involved, if I took the tape and demanded a little something for myself, I could probably get it. And that might mean the kind of freedom where I could truly start my life again.

It was not going to be easy though; I would need help. And of course I knew someone who would do anything for me, especially because of what he had to lose with the tape. I turned the video into a computer file and sent it off to Dejan, with a short message and my Toronto phone number. I said we should talk about forgiveness and what it would take.

On the phone, I made it clear it was not going to be easy. It would require him to play things as though he was determined to get the tape and eliminate me, and with two men who had known him for a long time. But now of course Dejan doesn't have to act anymore, his hunt for me is real.

I was foolish and desperate. Put it down to the lure of real closure. There would be no trace of the old Nataša. A whole new me could emerge who bore no trace of who I was before.

I was seduced by my own faith in my shape-shifting. Well, the seduction is finally over. It's time to act, clear-eyed, with the small amount of integrity I have left.

35. Lucien Bollinger

The crowd of theatregoers had begun to amass at the front doors, dressed as if for a wedding. There were cordial nods and smiles among the grey-haired patrons. I glimpsed the tanned, freckled arm of an older woman tucked closely into the crook of her husband's elbow as they came out of a cab. The husband slipped among his kind, and they all looked sleek as seals in their freshly pressed dark suits. One liver-spotted hand pulled a twenty off a brass money clip and handed it to the kid selling roses—it was a gesture only a man who had lived with real money all his life would make.

Another wave started to pour through the doors. One by one, the taxis glided and slowed to a stop and emptied out the younger couples making a date night of it. Cheeks flushed from pre-show champagne, the women hobbled in new heels with their lumbering business-casual boyfriends. The men stared coldly straight ahead, like big dogs being taken to the kennel.

I stood among the rest of those still hopeful for a ticket, taking my place in the line that formed in seconds. I wished I had one of my cameras. It was all such cheap theatre outside, but I had a feeling it might be more authentic than what I was about to see.

That's when I saw him. He drove by in a white car with tinted windows. It looked to be another cheap rental, one chosen from the lot because it was as non-descript as possible. He had rolled down the window on the passenger side to get a good look at who was going into the theatre. He had that same look I remembered - a death's head come to life.

Did he see me see him? I was not going to stand around and find out. He was after Nataša and she had to be inside.

I moved to the doors in an effort to glimpse who had made it in. I was too purposeful, I could tell I was making the usher nervous. He took a tentative half-step to the right to block the entrance behind him.

"Can I help you?"

"Just looking for my wife. She's got my ticket."

"Oh. That's unfortunate." He frowned. The ruby stud in his nostril glistened. "Can you call her?"

"I'm going to try, but I think she turned her phone off. Could I . . ."

"I'm sorry. You can't." Three stragglers breezed past me, tickets in hand. They kept the usher distracted, his fingers nimbly touching the tickets offered, scanning the letters and numbers.

I glanced up at the people taking the stairs to the balcony seats. And suddenly couldn't breathe: Nataša, in profile, in a bright red dress. Her hair had been dyed a coppery blonde, but it was her, no question.

"Nataša!"

She turned, and the frightened, startled look in those dark eyes immediately softened. But she did not smile. She slowly blinked and it was hard to know whether she was feeling relief at the sight of me or a sudden wave of sadness. I watched her lips move and form my name as she slowly began to descend the stairs, coming my way.

The older members of the crowd around me were giving me stern looks. The vulgarity of me, shouting in a place like this.

They cleared a space around me, as if I might be prone to sudden violent gestures.

I nodded to the ticket taker as if to say see? I told you! I slipped through the couple ahead of me, raising my finger to tell him I would just be a second, all would be resolved once I had gotten to her.

"Lucien, what are you doing?"

I took her in my arms. Damn the looks from those around us. She was alive, she was there, I could make her mine again. As I kissed her I realized her eyes were wide open and she had begun to struggle to break free from my embrace.

"Not here. How did you know?"

"Milan! I remembered Milan, the name. The guy directing this, he's that Uncle Milan of yours, isn't he? I knew you'd have to be here. I can't tell you . . . I was losing my mind."

"You can't be here."

She had stepped back from my embrace and her eyes were on those approaching. She smiled weakly. It seemed a reflex, a way to tell those around us it was okay. *This man's not dangerous.* I suppose it was something one learned spending time with violent men.

I felt a strong hand on my arm, another on my shoulder. I turned, and my new friends were not the pale fops in tux shirts and bowties like the usher. These were big boys in security uniforms, steroid muscle going to flab. With a practised air of calm, as if they had come to soothe me, they took my arms and began to move me along.

"I'm sorry, sir. I'm afraid you can't—"

"Nataša, I've just seen him. Dejan. He's here. He was in a car, he cruised by. I swear it was him."

She nodded, as if in resignation. After pulling out of my arms, she had locked herself into an icy calm.

"You should wait for me out front, okay? There is a party afterwards. I'll take you there and we can talk."

I nodded to her as they turned me around and marched me to the door. I broke free of the security guards once I had gotten past the velour rope, stumbling from the force of them pushing me out onto the street.

The cops. Now I had a reason to go to them. Nataša was in danger. Nobody here was going to listen to me, of course. Not after this. But I had held her in my arms! Every horrible minute of our days apart was worth it for the feeling of pulling her close again. No one—not even Dejan—was going to drive her away from me now.

Somewhere on the street I knew there would be a police cruiser. I would flag the first one down. The thought of calling 911 and trying to explain the situation and to say . . . what, there might be an emergency? At best they would try to calm me down and advise me to talk to a security guard. Best to figure it out myself. With the way I was dressed and the fact that I was lucid and sober—that had to mean something in this part of town.

But it was clearly going to take longer than I imagined. I had walked about ten minutes from the theatre when I realized the neighbourhood had changed. There were rusted bars on windows, bruised fruit stacked on a rickety stall, a worried look on the other side of the display window of a convenience store, taking me in like I might be a thief. I passed a hotel where an emaciated figure in a short skirt and halter top turned to grin at me. There was the wail of a cruiser and then a fire truck, but they sounded like they were blocks from where I was and only speeding farther away.

Not even Parkdale on a full moon night got quite like this. The tattooed arms of a biker in a wheelchair pumped as he glided by me, sizing me up. "Need some blow?" he whispered. A kid long ago lost to crystal meth, in surfer shorts, his skinny legs flecked with fresh scars, turned and lurched from left to right on the wide avenue, barking out curses. I glanced down an alleyway and there, by a battered green dumpster, were two men dressed in hoodies, looking like hermit monks. They were not smoking though; they were fixing up, tying off, squatting on a rusted loading dock. One took me in with a heavy-lidded nod, brushing away a grey dreadlock from his eyes. They could have been forty, fifty, sixty, it was hard to tell. It must have been like living in a time-lapse film, aging out there, the hours, days and months consumed in the quest for moments of peace in these hideaway places, safe from the threat of a blade, the demand for your beggar's change.

Then I felt the impact of flesh slamming into me and stumbled back. Two huge forearms, swathed in a camouflage jacket, thumped against my chest to knock me further. I fell but managed to slap my hands down and break the impact before my head snapped back on the concrete. Before me was a man who must have been close to seven feet tall. His shiny black hair hung loose down to the middle of his chest.

"You rush me? Want to try something?"

"I'm so sorry. I wasn't looking."

He lifted me up and I guess he couldn't help but smile at the incongruity of me in this neighbourhood in my formal clothes.

"You better be looking. You shouldn't be down here."

I looked down at the palms of my hands, scraped red and bleeding. "I'm looking for the police."

"The cops? Why you need the cops? You get rolled?"

"Not yet. I . . ."

"Better get your hands washed and clean up some place. You should head on back the way I'm going. You don't want to be down here. City of the walking dead, man. The cops don't go by here that often unless they have to."

"I need to talk to one."

He gave me a slow look up and down, considering me carefully. Then he reached into the pocket of his jacket and pulled out a cell phone. He nodded to me to follow him.

As we walked out of the neighbourhood he murmured into the phone. I felt my palms start to ache, the skin raw, little pearls of blood appearing where the skin had torn. He was oblivious to me glumly marching a step behind him. He was far more interested in what the voice on the other end of the line was saying. He started to chuckle, and I was convinced he and whoever was on the other end of the line were laughing at my foolishness.

We came to a corner where the buildings rose about ten stories. There were trees in concrete boxes on the sidewalk lining the route back to the neighbourhood of the theatre. I felt a sudden sense of calm. Dusk had turned to night, and the stars were visible over the tops of those new condo towers in the distance.

"You wait here at this corner. Cop's coming for you."

"Thanks, man."

The big man tilted his head and furrowed his brow, as if he was not quite sure he had heard me correctly. He waited until he was a few metres away on the sidewalk to raise his hand like a wave without looking back. I stood holding my palms up as if I had been asked for change. I could feel the beat of my heart all the way down to my wrists.

It wasn't long before a cruiser glided to a stop in front of me and the cop in the passenger side waved me over. I heard the metal thump of the lock disengaging in the door as the cop motioned for me to get in the back seat.

"Looks like you got into a scrape, eh?" The cop reached into the glove compartment and pulled out a first-aid kit in a blue plastic box. He pulled out two Band-Aids and slid them to me through a slot in the Plexiglas screen that separated the front seat from the back. "Want to put your ID in there?"

The cop beside him in the driver's seat was a bigger man,

young, who looked like he had just joined the force. He stared straight ahead with a stubbled frown, listening, trying to appear as indifferent as possible.

"I was at the theatre, officer, then I went down that way, looking for you guys."

"Us guys?"

"The police, sir. There's a woman in danger. There at the theatre, I mean."

The younger cop was grinning. He looked over at his partner—they'd laugh about this one later. His partner gave my driver's licence a quick scan and then put it back through the slot.

"What you doing here in Vancouver, Mister Bollinger?"

"I came here to find her. This woman. Nataša Ružić."

"The woman at the theatre."

"That's right."

"And why might Nataša Ružić be in trouble?"

"She's from Bosnia. There are some Serbian people who want her dead. Or maybe one guy, I don't know. "

The two cops traded a quick, furtive glance. The younger shook his head.

"Is Nataša your girlfriend?'

"I don't know right now. I mean she ran away and she wouldn't . . ."

"She ran away."

The kid cop was now punching letters into the little screen that swivelled out from the middle of the dashboard. "How you spelling Nataša, sir?"

"Just with an S."

"You sure about that?"

"You can check it yourself. Google for the newspaper stories on Alex Rebane's murder in Toronto. She disappeared that night."

"She's disappeared but now she's at the theatre."

The kid cop turned to his partner, shook his head with a goofy smile. Whatever.

"I swear to you. She's in danger. Check out her name. Ružić. Missing person."

"You know how many missing persons we get told are coming through Van every week, Mr. Bollinger? I'm not saying I don't believe you. I'm not saying she's not in danger. That all might be true. I'm telling you we're not going to bust into that theatre and put a halt to a show people paid good money for to find your friend. They've got a smart team of security guards working in there. They know how to spot any trouble before it happens. We'll call this in, how's that?"

I sank into the back seat. It smelled a bit like bug spray back there. I wanted to wail out my rage, there must have been something about the ambience, shall we say, of the cage of Plexiglas and reinforced steel I was in. I nodded as meekly as possible. Nothing left to do but work around these fools.

"Now we can drop you off at your hotel or we can let you go here. But if we do that you've got to promise me you're not going to make anybody's life difficult tonight."

"It's fine, officer. I won't cause anyone any trouble."

The older cop turned and gave me his coldest stare. "You sure about that now?"

"I'm sure."

"'Cause we take you downtown, you're in for a whole world of hurt. You look like a good guy. You got an honest face. How'll be you get yourself a coffee right there, then you come back once the play's over, tell your sweetheart the cops in Vancouver are nice guys. Guys you can talk to if you're in any trouble."

"I'll do that, officer."

"You really should."

The lock in the door beside me thumped open. I took my cue and made my exit. "Thank you, officer."

"Enjoy your stay in Vancouver, Mr. Bollinger."

And then the cruiser glided away down the street. I paused to look at the brake lights when it slowed to a stop. The two cops were hunched, hooded shadows. Their silhouettes had amber, then popsicle red auras around them. I figured they wouldn't be back my way any time soon.

As I re-entered the lobby I could hear, behind the heavy doors, a woman's voice, loud and bold as opera. The lobby was deserted save for an old woman wearing a black lace dress—like a funeral gown—emerging from the ladies' room. Her gaze was focused somewhere past the standing bar. If I could just slip in a door up on the balcony level where Nataša was, maybe I could find an empty seat.

I climbed the stairs and realized there was another usher watching me closely. I did not acknowledge her, I continued with my performance of someone returning to his seat. I marched to an aisle entrance, my gaze fixed on the caramel coloured hexagons of the carpet design.

It was the sheer power of the voice declaiming that compelled me to look up. There on a stage that was bare but for a wide corridor of broken columns, backlit to create long shadows at her feet, was a young woman that could have been Nataša's sister. Her dark hair hung loose in long, heavy ringlets, and her eyes were painted like Cleopatra's, with thick black lines around her eyelids. She wore nothing more than a shift stained with splotches of fake blood. There was fear in her eyes. I stood frozen, a few steps from the entrance to the aisle. I was transfixed. It felt like she was gazing solely at me.

"Your seat, sir?"

It was the usher, sounding as polite as possible, really. She led me back out of the theatre.

"I thought I was . . ."

"Where's your ticket?"

I padded my front pocket and shook my head. It was not a bad act. But it seemed like the usher had seen this one before. All her impatience was distilled in the way that she wearily blinked, her gaze on my hands. "I must have thrown it out at intermission."

"You never had one. I recognize you now. From before the show."

I sharply exhaled, as if I had a right to be exasperated.

"You don't want me to call security. I don't want to call security." She was speaking so slowly but firmly. There were faint summer freckles along her nose. "If you just exit now, I won't have to."

"All right, all right. I'm going."

I turned and began to descend the stairs. A final thought to save a shred of dignity came to me, and I looked back to address her, though I was not quite courageous enough to make eye contact. "Somebody might be in danger in there, I'm telling you."

The usher had already turned her back on me. I watched her calmly return to the aisles.

Outside, I stood in front of the theatre. It had begun to rain. I had depleted my last reserves of resistance—I had to have a cigarette. The wind had picked up, and the wisp of flame in my lighter flickered out once, twice, third time lucky. Whatever luck might have meant by then.

It was the quiet that was unnerving. Why did it seem that even the street outside had gotten still before the end of the show? Another blast of wind, beaded with cold rain, sent a chill through me. I couldn't shake the distinct sense that I was being watched. Dejan had to be somewhere, but there seemed no vantage point for him to take me in. The parked cars? The windows on the sec-

ond and third floors of an old sandstone office building next door?
All those windows were closed, with the blinds pulled down. No,
I was skittish and adrenalized. I feared that I had only come so
close to watch Nataša slip away from me for good.

*Why would she not want to be found? Why would she not want to be
rescued from Dejan and whatever danger she's in?* These were the questions that had never occurred to me when I made the decision to
get on that plane. Now I saw that my denial of the very possibility
of these questions had led me to react so strongly to the thought
of her sitting through the performance alone. Perhaps in my heart
I didn't really believe she was in any danger. The only thing in
danger now was my faith that she might actually still care for me.

"Look at you, silly man. You come to my rescue."

I turned and there she was, with that smile that I remembered.
She had slipped out early and had brushed open the door behind
me. She reached for me, and here was the embrace that I had
hoped for. The gentle music of her laugh.

"Nataša. Oh God . . . You have no idea."

"No, my love." She gently tapped me on the nose with the tip
of her finger. "It is you who have no idea."

"Are you all right?"

"Do I look all right?" She brushed a hand across her bangs and
raised one eyebrow, a parody of flirtation.

"You're not scared to be out here in public? I just saw Dejan. I
think he's stalking you."

She nodded, with a look of sad resignation I remembered from
our last days together in Toronto. "You seem scared enough for
both of us, no?"

"Shouldn't I be? We have to get the police involved."

She patted down the lapels I had pulled up to shield myself
from the rain. "You think? You don't have anything to worry
about. With me, well, we'll see."

"What do you mean?"

She smiled, clasped my hand. She slipped a small white ticket into my bandaged palm. "What happened to you?"

"I fell. It's not important. I'm fine."

"This is a ticket for the after-party. You must come with me. You can meet Milan. All this will be explained for you, how's that?"

"I'd prefer to hear it from you. Alone."

She pulled me tightly to her once more. "But that's not possible, Lucien. Be here for me now. It is all I ask."

"You're all I ask for."

As we kissed, I didn't know whether to take comfort in the fact there were tears in her eyes. "Please. Don't say such things right now."

She led me back into the lobby as the crowd was streaming out into the street. I could feel the warmth of her hand in mine as I put on my best face of serene confidence.

I pressed her hand and leaned close to her ear to speak low. "Listen, you have to know I'm not crazy, getting on the plane."

She raised her hand and caught the bartender's eye, a crisp twenty-dollar bill rolled up in her fingers. "Two glasses of red, please."

"Nataša, Petar and Caroline, they are gone too. Murdered, like Alex."

She nodded as she watched the wine splash into the first glass. "That would suggest some kind of connection to me, you think?"

I tried to summon up a laugh, but it didn't come. "Nataša, you heard what I said. Petar and Caroline."

"Of course I heard you, yes. I've been reading and watching the news. I haven't shut myself off from the world."

"You know how many times I tried to contact you? Any kind of response at all . . ."

The bartender served us our glasses of wine, and Nataša sang a coquettish little thank you for him. So strange, the instant change in her mood, it was like she had flicked to another TV station in her head.

"It's a long story. I had to write it all down for myself first. It took me days. Thank God your country's so big, I had the time to finish."

"Why couldn't you respond to me, tell me you were okay?"

"That would have been dangerous, no? That would have told everybody where I was. I needed to disappear, Lucien. At least until I got here."

She walked away from the bar, leading me in the direction of the cordoned-off area where the after-party had begun.

"It all ends here, Lucien. Here. Tonight."

I trailed behind her as she held my hand so tenderly. The lightest touch on my fingertips.

"What's ending, Nataša? You're making me worried. More worried than I was before I got here."

"As I said, you have nothing to worry about, believe me." She turned to me as we handed our tickets over. Her fingers fluttered against mine again. "This is how I used to lead my customers to the VIP section, when I danced for them."

"Just answer me. What's finishing? You mean us?'

"I never danced for you, did I? Would you have wanted that?"

"Nataša, please don't talk in the past tense."

"Lucien, it's not just us. I'm talking in the past tense about everything." She gently caressed the nape of my neck and kissed me. "It's not you. You were never . . . You were clean, do you understand me? When I first saw you, that's what I could tell. You had a clean soul."

"I don't think I know what that means."

"No? May that always be the case."

214

She took me by the hand through the crowd, and there, across the room, was a shaggy guy who had to be in his sixties. The dark rings around his eyes made him look like an old basset hound. The woman beside him had the dyed blond streaks of her hair pulled back into a tight, shiny bun, like an old ballerina. She was in a dark silk dress that affirmed the sense of formality her date seemed so eager to deny. There was not a wrinkle on her, not even on her bronzed face. The man had his hands held out to take Nataša's as he beamed for her across the room. And at that moment I recognized him—Milan, the director from the newspaper article.

"There you are, there you are at last."

Nataša took his hands in hers and looked into his eyes like a lover. They didn't embrace. It was as much affection as she could expend.

"Milan, Mira, let me introduce you to Lucien Bollinger. He's my date from Toronto."

They nodded and said their greetings and pleasantries to me. Mira looked me up and down like a mother-in-law.

"So you saw it, my work. Our work." He looked to Mira for forgiveness of his slip, and she shook her head. It was a battle she had long given up on, it was clear, making him remember the efforts of others around him. "How was it?"

"It was much as I expected. I mean that in the best way, Milan."

He turned to me and gave me a tug at my elbow. "You know I told her when we met a few days ago, I cast my Cassandra after her. She was quite an actress when she was younger."

"I still am, Milan."

"I'm sure, I'm sure." His laugh trailed off abruptly when he realized no one was joining him. He knit his brow for a moment, looked down at the carpet. He was not used to people letting him laugh alone, and it was puzzling him. "Very talented family. Did she tell you her father was a writer, Mr. Bollinger?"

"She did not, no."

I looked to Nataša, but her eyes were fixed on Milan. Her smile had gone rigid, like it was an act of will now.

"He made films too. I produced one of his plays—"

"Uncle Milan, maybe we can talk about this some other time?"

"It was brilliant."

"Milan. Stop. You saw the news of the arrest of that man Nikola Lazarević here? Everything, the death of that artist in Toronto. It's all connected. Connected to me."

Mira frowned. "You should go to the police!"

"It's not so simple. I'll need a lawyer. I'll need to explain myself as best I can or else . . . but I'm worried for us here. I'm worried for you both. Can we please go somewhere, someplace private? I hate to do this to you. This is your night, but I feel there is no choice. Something bad . . ."

Milan was looking around at the guests who were moving in their own circles, decorously giving the great director his privacy. He seemed to shrink inside his suit, saddened by all of this, saddened and shaken. His hand trembled as he held his wine glass.

"Mira, this is necessary. Come, let's leave. Come, let's go and discuss things at our place here."

We moved quickly through the lobby. Milan and Mira smiled for those who recognized the great director and his muse and simply had to congratulate them. With whatever shambling charm he could muster he thanked the well-wishers for them both, and mimed that he had to go out for a cigarette. Nataša wouldn't even look at me. She had retracted into a state of troubling serenity.

As we walked out into the street it felt like the temperature had dropped. The wind had picked up force with the rain. I trailed behind the three of them, more unsure and fearful with each step. I wanted to grab Nataša's arm, pull her back. She kept marching two steps ahead, as if, like a tour guide, she was moving us all forward into the night.

That's when I saw Dejan's white car again, speeding to the corner we had passed. I glimpsed his dark silhouette in the driver's seat. He ran the stop sign at the corner and barrelled through toward us. He pulled up onto the curb and leapt out, the car still running.

I guess I knew this would be decisive, but I wasn't conscious of thinking it through in the moment. I have no memory of moving for the car first as Dejan grabbed Nataša. I do remember her scream, how it propelled me toward them.

Dejan turned with Nataša, gripping her arms. His shoulders were hunched, he was poised to barge right through Milan and Mira and get back to the car. As he neared them Milan raised his hand, a halting gesture more than anything. With one arm still firmly gripping Nataša, Dejan struck him down and then turned, reaching for his crotch. Mira cried out "Milan!" and shrunk from Dejan, holding her face in her hands.

Nataša screamed once more as the gun appeared. And that's when I moved. I bolted for Dejan, who had his back turned to me. I threw myself toward him, and we both fell to the street. His gun clattered as it landed on the road beyond his reach. Nataša had broken free. She must have grabbed Mira and run for the crowd that had amassed around us a few yards away. There, behind them all, from the corner of my eye I saw the flashing red light of a police car, closer and closer.

Dejan jumped to his feet and kicked me once, twice. My arms were up, covering my face. He must have realized in that moment that his gun was too far. He couldn't finish me off as he'd have preferred. He cursed in Serbian and ran for his idling car.

Which wasn't idling anymore. I had his keys.

I remember the next moments as if they happened in slow

motion. His leaping into the car. I can only imagine the shocked look on his face; all of us heard his roar of outrage. The driver's door swung open. He turned his back to the crowd and he began to run.

He couldn't have gotten more than twenty or thirty metres from the car when two policemen had him. I watched him drop like a ragdoll to the pavement. They had him cuffed in seconds. He struggled for a few seconds and then, as they finally had him subdued, they pulled him up on his feet and roughly pulled him toward the cruiser. As his eyes met mine I held his car keys up. He looked broken and small.

I walked over to Nataša, but she turned away. She was focused on the cruiser, silent. "Thank God, you're all right."

I wanted to take her in my arms but she was rigid, determined to keep her distance. As the police cruiser drove away she turned to face me. She reached out and caressed my cheek. "You have your life, okay? Make it good."

She turned from me and walked toward the second police car. Milan called to her but she didn't respond. She said a few words to a couple of policemen who were standing by the crowd, trying to question witnesses. One of the officers nodded, and then they escorted her to their car, where she got in the back seat. I watched the tail lights of the cruiser get smaller and smaller down the street.

I looked down at the palms of my shaking hands. New spots of deep red blood beaded there. I reached out to those approaching, shaking my head, trying to find the words. But no words came.

36. Dejan Vidić

I'll admit I fucked up. I hate guns. This one, I got it in Chinatown for five hundred bucks. I haven't shot one in years.

It was too late. It was all closing in.

We could have made a life, she and I. I swear to you that's all I wanted.

Fucking culture. What's that saying? Every time I hear the word it makes me want to reach for my gun.

Foča made no sense. Shitty little village. We had higher priorities.

That summer. So fucking hot. We never talked about those days, and when I say we I mean all the guys who were in the forces back in those days.

But Foča. No, we had to go there. Special orders. That's all Nikola said.

I never asked him about that. Maybe he didn't know anything anyway. Maybe he was just following orders. Or maybe he had a sense of what was going on all along.

That was her belief. She said her mother's death in Foča . . . that was in nobody's interest. It was her father who had to die that day, and which she would never forgive.

She said she actually believed Milan might be her real father.

She said she wanted to be a butterfly. I still don't know what that means.

I fucking loved that butterfly though, and there she was.

There she was; she was gone.

37. Christina Perretti

I heard she is now awaiting her trial. Given what we discovered during the course of our investigation, that seemed unsurprising. That scene in front of the theatre . . . It was like an immigrant's version of a bad American movie.

I knew it was her who killed Alex Rebane, not Vidić. No one agreed with me about that. And yet it was so clear to me; it did not even need explaining.

But I will leave it to them all to figure out why now. They are good people, but they do terrible police work over there. Stumbling in the dark.

Now I've got more than enough work with what I now know of Barany and his network. Perhaps I'm not stumbling so much anymore myself.

38. Lucien Bollinger

The plane broke through the clouds as it began its descent towards Pearson. I looked out the window, and way down there the grid had a coppery glow, the city's micro-circuitry of streets pulsing with the pin-point headlights of cars. *Try to see things in a new way*; this was my working maxim now.

And maybe that desire to see things anew was what led me to the paintings of Alex Rebane in the first place. For years, I believed I could become a photographer, and I had allowed myself to drift in a state of incurious reliance on received perceptions, received ideas. Work like Alex's provided a way to distinguish such a fabric of disguise from the real thing.

The real thing once in my life and now gone, of course. It feels like Nataša has left me forever. She saved me when I struggled to understand the difference between the one desired and the one who is truly loved. Things were too far along by the time I could finally see clearly, and yet really, how could I have expected any more from myself? How could it have gone any other way? If going after what was real was my downfall, well, I am at peace with my descent.

"Please take your seat and fasten your seat belt, and ensure your seat back and folding trays are in their full upright position."

I'd had five hours on the flight to assess what I might still make of my life. There might be some freelance photography work I could eventually get, but if I was honest with myself, even before I had met Alex Rebane I was losing faith in the digitized image to express anything with the power of, say, a Caravaggio or a Gentileschi, work of such baroque drama that it inspired Alex to create. I was starting to imagine what it might be like to explore that kind of artifice, to shape a vision out of what I had learned about Nataša's life from Milan and Mira over my last few days in Vancouver. It would take the kind of single-mindedness and courage that Alex Rebane had had, and I'm still not sure I can summon that kind of blind faith in myself.

On the flight I read a magazine article, written in the breathless prose of a bad press release, about a new website available to view on all the little screens we carry around with us. The writer was predicting that virtually every home video and every film ever produced could eventually be up online. We will cannibalize every scrap of moving image, desperately searching for what was once authentic. And I am not above that impulse. The first thing I resolved to do upon returning home was to digitize all my old photographs, including the ones I took of my father's Holland. Those images were not real to him, they were nothing compared to his memory; perhaps he was actually right about that.

I think of the currency Nataša gave to the power of the image, how she spent the last days of her freedom trying to elude those from her past and erase all images of herself, starting with those that Alex painted of her. It was a heroic, doomed attempt at transformation, an act of revenge on fate as much on those who had fixed her image in memory. She was not made for this century.

It was close to ten when the taxi pulled up in front of my place. The building before me looked smaller than when I had left it, the red of the bricks darker in the glow of the one streetlight. The leaves on the struggling little Japanese maple had already started to turn. It must have gotten colder while I was away.

As I opened the door and flicked on the light, I saw a parcel among the few bills and bank statements that had been dropped through the door. There was no return address. I walked over to the kitchen and tore it open with a knife. There, wrapped in newspaper, a poor man's present, was a video camera and four notebooks, with numbers and places scrawled on each cover in black felt pen.

There was a note from Nataša.

Lucien,

I am sorry I had to leave you there as I did. I don't think I am the person you came to have feelings for. In these notebooks I tried to capture who I really am. I don't need them anymore. I give them to you.

I did not write in these pages about what happened to Alex. It was me who destroyed those paintings as well. My first act of seeking some justice, I suppose: to erase myself.

I am nowhere in the video in that camera. All I shot were empty spaces and stretches of highway at night, nothing but the blurry white constellations of headlights in the distance. No humans.

These books are peopled by my past. I want you to read them now not because I want your forgiveness. If I am to be forgiven for what I have done—not least what happened to Alex—I know I must be tried and judged in a court of law like everyone else, and that is what I must prepare for now. I may not see you for a long time, maybe years, but that is justice. More than anything else, if I am to live with myself, this is what I must believe in.

But I did believe in us. If you remember anything about me, believe that.

With love,

Nataša

So I opened the first notebook. I struggled out of my suit jacket, slung it over the kitchenette chair. And then I sat down and began to read.

39. Alex Rebane

Dear M.,

Las Vegas. How you would have loved this desert city. I think of how you rendered card sharps, cheats, and whores, all the drama of a good con distilled in those moments of the basest transactions. It's all here, millions poured into air-conditioned cathedrals for the worship of sudden dumb luck.

You probably would have stayed away from the hotel I'm in, though, preferring humbler accommodations. I imagine you with a disdain for pomp and artifice, that intuitive distrust of wealth because it corrupts. After too much wine you'd want an argument about it, and you would have bored me with your insistence on what was real as the focus of a painter's vocation.

Still, you would have taken their money if they had asked you to paint a fresco here, wouldn't you have? Because money meant freedom, right? It could lift you above everything, including a murder charge. Well, the more things change . . .

Here I am, the guest of a couple of my patrons, at an art fair ostensibly selling my work, but really I think I'm looking for inspiration, looking for something—or should I say someone?—to paint.

And I think I found her. She is the assistant of Caroline, who is not just one of the rich who keeps me working, but also my confidante of sorts. Caroline introduced me to a Nataša Rubik or Rujik last night.

And she is like a Rubik's cube, this one, like those puzzles that frustrated me as a boy trying to line up those little coloured cubes correctly. Mondrian would have loved it. The woman, Nataša, fascinates me, and I think I'm in love (well . . . you know what I mean).

She has a toughened, impish beauty, eyes that light up with passion and then dim as soon as you start to bore her—as the dinner guests, old Hong Kong millionaires that Caroline insisted we had to dine with, clearly did. Nataša has literally been through a war, has come back from hell, and yet carries her wisdom so lightly, so elegantly. Maybe she's thirty, but really she could be ageless.

For years I've had a secret wish to do something with the Orpheus myth, transform it like you would have, finding your own underworld in the Rome you were living in.

Last night, walking home from dinner in a theme-park version of Rome, where all the streets have been meticulously recreated and turned into a shopping mall, Caroline and I were deep in conversation, and I turned back to look at Nataša and, well, maybe it was the ambience of the fake via Condotti, but she looked like I have always imagined Eurydice, walking two steps behind through the underworld.

And now I simply have to paint her this way. I must talk to Caroline as soon as I can and figure out a way this can happen. I would need a week with her in my studio. This feels like the most urgent directive I've received in years from my painter brain. I better listen, don't you think? Before, like Eurydice, she simply disappears before my eyes.

Yours,

A.